# The Blazing-World

# THE
# Description
OF A NEW
# World
CALLED
# The Blazing-World

WRITTEN
By the Thrice Noble, Illustrious, and Excellent
PRINCESSE
Margaret Cavendish
The Duchess of Newcastle

First published in 1666
Introduction © 2020 by Ian Randal Strock

This modern production maintains, as much as possible, the author's original spellings, and only updates the typography for ease of reading.

This is a work of fiction. All the characters and events portrayed in this book are either fictitious or are used fictitiously.

All rights reserved. Printed in the United States of America. No part of this publication may be reproduced, stored in a retrieval system, or transmitted in any form or by any means, digital, electronic, mechanical, photocopying, recording, or otherwise, or conveyed via the internet or a website without prior written permission of the publisher, except in the case of brief quotations embodied in critical articles and reviews.

Gray Rabbit Publications
1380 East 17 Street, Suite 2233
Brooklyn, New York 11230
www.FantasticBooks.biz

Simultaneous hardcover and trade paperback publication

| Hardcover | Trade Paperback |
|---|---|
| ISBN 10: 1-5154-2415-4 | ISBN 10: 1-5154-2416-2 |
| ISBN 13: 978-1-5154-2415-4 | ISBN 13: 978-1-5154-2416-1 |

First Gray Rabbit Edition, 2020

# *Introduction*

*The Description of a New World Called the Blazing-World*, according to author Margaret Cavendish, was written "as an appendix to my *Observations upon Experimental Philosophy*." However, seeking a wider audience (she regrets that "by reason most Ladies take no delight in Philosophical Arguments"), she separated out this story to be presented on its own.

Describing the book she claims "the first part is romancical; the second, philosophical, and the third, merely fancy, or "fantastical."

In her epilogue, Cavendish writes that it is not her ambition to be empress, but that she aspires to the much higher calling of being "authoress of a whole world." She notes that the creation of the Blazing World and the Philosophical World was more easily and quickly done than the conquests of Alexander the Great or Julius Caesar. She also takes pride in not having made as many disturbances, nor caused as many deaths, as Alexander or Caesar, while taking "more delight and glory" in her creation than they did in the creations of their empires.

Cavendish's view of utopia, her Blazing-World, is peaceful because it has "but one religion, one language, and one government." It is those factions and divisions, and their resultant wars, which she assumes is the cause of dystopia. And thus, since she "esteems peace before war, wit before policy, and honesty before beauty," she chooses instead to be her greatest idol, "Honest Margaret Newcastle."

Cavendish did not consider herself poor, nor did she seek great wealth or even power. She writes "I should desire only so much as might suffice to repair my... husband's losses." Her ambition, she continues, is to be the creator of a world, which she has done with this book.

Modern scholars have described the book as "a hermaphroditic text," because Cavendish confronts $17^{th}$ century norms regarding science, politics, gender, and identity. Nicole Pohl of Oxford Brookes University, for example, says that Cavendish's willingness to question her society's conceptions while discussing such "male" topics allowed her to move into a gender-neutral discussion of them, creating what Pohl labels, "a truly emancipatory poetic space."

Cavendish was one of the few female authors of her time to write and publish under her own name, rather than anonymously or pseudonymously. Marina Leslie of Northeastern University says that remembering Cavendish's role as an early feminist is as important as remembering that the utopian genre itself was brand new. Leslie says used the utopian genre to discuss issues such as "female nature and authority" in a new light, while simultaneously expanding the utopian genre itself.

Oddvar Holmesland of the University of Edinburgh writes "the term 'hybridization' aptly captures Cavendish's method of blending established genres and categories into a new order, and of presenting her fantasy empire as versimilar."

Sujata Iyengar of the University of Georgia compliments Cavendish's use of fiction as a counterpoint to her *Observations upon Experimental Philosophy* (1666), noting that writing a work of fiction allowed her to "explore ideas of rank, gender, and race that directly clash with commonly held beliefs about servility in her era." Additionally, the freedom afforded by writing fiction gave her an opportunity to explore ideas that directly conflict with those in her nonfiction writing.

Politically, Cavendish echoes her contemporary, philosopher Thomas Hobbes. Cavendish's Empress of The Blazing-World asserts that a it is the lack of societal divisions that leads to a peaceful society. And that, to eliminate those divisions and maintain social harmony, a monarchical government is the only possible choice. Only absolute sovereignty, Cavendish argues, can maintain social unity and stability because the reliance on one authority eliminates separations of power. She bolsters her argument, writing "it was natural for one body to have one head, so it was also natural for a politic body to have but one governor… besides, said they, a monarchy is a divine form of government, and agrees most with our religion."

Hobbes, in his *Leviathan* (which was published 15 years before *The Blazing-World*), says that a monarchical government is a necessary force in preventing societal instability and ruin.

### *Margaret Cavendish*

Margaret Lucas was born in 1623, the youngest of eight children. She had no formal education, but her family—more financially secure than most—did give her access to libraries and tutors. Her father died when she was fairly young, but—she writes in her 1656 autobiography—her mother was able to keep the family in a condition "not much lower" than when her father was alive. And the children kept their access to "honest pleasures and harmless delights."

When Queen Henrietta Maria was in Oxford (in 1643), Margaret's mother gave permission for her to become one of the Queen's Ladies-in-waiting. The following year, Margaret went with the Queen into her exile in France. Having been accustomed to hiding her intelligence—as social mores dictated—to all beyond her family, Margaret found herself very bashful and uncomfortable in France, her first time away from her family. She asked to leave the court, but her mother persuaded her to stay, rather than disgrace herself by leaving.

In 1645, she married William Cavendish, the Marquess of Newcastle, who was thirty years her senior (she was his second wife). She later wrote that her husband liked her bashfulness, and that he was the only man she was ever in love with, loving him not for title, wealth or power, but for merit, justice, gratitude, duty, and fidelity. Margaret had no children, though William came to the marriage with five surviving children from his first marriage.

In *The Life of the Thrice Noble, High and Puissant Prince William Cavendishe* (1667), the biography she wrote of her husband, she spoke of a time when there were rumors that her husband actually wrote the works which are credited to her. She notes that her husband defended her amidst those accusations. She also said there was a creative relationship with her husband, and that he was her writing tutor.

In the first years of their marriage, Margaret and her brother-in-law, Sir Charles Cavendish, returned to England, hoping to receive the proceeds of the sale of her husband's estate (which had been confiscated due to his being a royalist delinquent). They were denied, and after a year, she left England again to be with her husband.

Writing in *A True Relation of My Birth, Breeding, and Life* (1656), Margaret said that her bashful nature, or "melancholia," made her "repent my going from home to see the World abroad." She was reluctant to talk about her work in public.

She did, however, enjoy reinventing herself through fashion. She said that she aimed for uniqueness in her dress, thoughts, and behavior, and that she disliked wearing the same fashions as other women. And she made no secret of her desire to be famous, though she expected to be criticized for writing a memoir, which she did "so that later generations would have a true account of her lineage and life."

In 1665, William was created the first Duke of Newcastle upon Tyne, making Margaret a Duchess. Margaret died, childless, on December 15, 1673. Her husband survived her by three years.

Other major works by Margaret Cavendish include:

*Poems and Fancies* (1653): a collection of poems, epistles, and some prose.

*Nature's Pictures drawn by Fancy's Pencil to the Life* (1656): an attempt to combine modes and genres, it includes the short prose romances "The Contract" and "Assaulted and Pursued Chastity," as well as several prefatory addresses to the reader.

*A True Relation of my Birth, Breeding, and Life* (1656): an autobiographical memoir.

*Orations* (1662): a collection.

*Philosophical Letters* (1664): a collection.

*CCXI Sociable Letters* (1664): a collection of letters as if composed by real women, discussing such topics as marriage, war, politics, medicine, science, and English and classical literature, as well as things like gambling and religious extremism.

*Observations upon Experimental Philosophy* (1666): in which she rejects Aristotelianism and mechanical philosophy in favor Stoic doctrines.

Two collections of her plays were published, in 1662 and 1668.

*—Ian Randal Strock*
*August 2020*

*Here on this Figure Cast a Glance.*
*But so as if it were by Chance,*
*Your eyes not fixt, they must not Stay,*
*Since this like Shadowes to the Day*
*It only represent's; for Still,*
*Her Beauty's found beyond the Skill*
*Of the best Paynter, to Imbrace*
*These lovely Lines within her face.*
*View her Soul's Picture, Judgment, witt,*
*Then read those Lines which Shee hath writt,*
*By Phancy's Pencill drawne alone*
*Which Peces but Shee, can justly owne.*

## Contents

To The Duchesse of Newcastle,
   On Her New Blazing-World.. . . . . . . . . . . . . . . . . . . . 13
To all Noble and Worthy Ladies.. . . . . . . . . . . . . . . . . . 15
The Description of a New World,
   Called The Blazing-World.. . . . . . . . . . . . . . . . . . 17
The Second Part of the
   Description of the New Blazing-World.. . . . . . . . . . . 85
The Epilogue to the Reader.. . . . . . . . . . . . . . . . . . . . 105

# To The Duchesse of Newcastle, On Her New Blazing-World.

*Our Elder World, with all their Skill and Arts,*
*Could but divide the World into three Parts:*
*Columbus, then for Navigation fam'd,*
*Found a new World, America 'tis nam'd;*
*Now this new World was found, it was not made,*
*Onely discovered, lying in Time's shade.*

*Then what are You, having no Chaos found*
*To make a World, or any such least ground?*
*But your Creating Fancy, thought it fit*
*To make your World of Nothing, but pure Wit.*
*Your Blazing-World, beyond the Stars mounts higher,*
*Enlightens all with a Cœlestial Fier.*

—William Newcastle.

## To all Noble and Worthy Ladies.

    This present *Description of a New World*, was made as an Appendix to my *Observations upon Experimental Philosophy*; and, having some Sympathy and Coherence with each other, were joyned together as Two several Worlds, at their Two Poles. But, by reason most Ladies take no delight in Philosophical Arguments, I separated some from the mentioned Observations, and caused them to go out by themselves, that I might express my Respects, in presenting to Them such Fancies as my Contemplations did afford. The First Part is Romancical; the Second, Philosophical; and the Third is meerly Fancy; or (as I may call it) Fantastical. And if (Noble Ladies) you should chance to take pleasure in reading these Fancies, I shall account my self a Happy Creatoress: If not, I must be content to live a Melancholly Life in my own World; which I cannot call a Poor World, if Poverty be only want of Gold, and Jewels: for, there is more Gold in it, than all the Chymists ever made; or, (as I verily believe) will ever be able to make. As for the Rocks of Diamonds, I wish, with all my Soul, they might be shared amongst my Noble Female Friends; upon which condition, I would willingly quit my Part: And of the Gold, I should desire only so much as might suffice to repair my Noble Lord and Husband's Losses: for, I am not Covetous, but as Ambitious as ever any of my Sex was, is, or can be; which is the cause, That though I cannot be Henry the Fifth, or Charles the Second; yet, I will endeavour to be, Margaret the First: and, though I have neither Power, Time nor Occasion, to be a great Conqueror, like Alexander, or Cesar; yet, rather than not be Mistress of a World, since Fortune and the Fates would give me none, I have made One of my own. And thus, believing, or, at least, hoping, that no Creature can, or will, Envy me for this World of mine, I remain,

    Noble Ladies, Your Humble Servant, M. Newcastle.

# The Description of a New World, Called The Blazing-World.

A Merchant travelling into a foreign Country, fell extreamly in Love with a young Lady; but being a stranger in that Nation, and beneath her, both in Birth and Wealth, he could have but little hopes of obtaining his desire; however his Love growing more and more vehement upon him, even to the slighting of all difficulties, he resolved at last to Steal her away; which he had the better opportunity to do, because her Father's house was not far from the Sea, and she often using to gather shells upon the shore accompanied not with above two to three of her servants it encouraged him the more to execute his design. Thus coming one time with a little leight Vessel, not unlike a Packet-boat, mann'd with some few Sea-men, and well victualled, for fear of some accidents, which might perhaps retard their journey, to the place where she used to repair; he forced her away: But when he fancied himself the happiest man of the World, he proved to be the most unfortunate; for Heaven frowning at his Theft, raised such a Tempest, as they knew not what to do, or whither to steer their course; so that the Vessel, both by its own leightness, and the violent motion of the Wind, was carried as swift as an Arrow out of a Bow, towards the North-pole, and in a short time reached the Icy Sea, where the wind forced it amongst huge pieces of Ice; but being little, and leight, it did by the assistance and favour of the gods to this virtuous Lady, so turn and wind through those precipices, as if it had been guided by some experienced Pilot, and skilful Mariner: But alas! Those few men which were in it, not knowing whither they went, nor what was to be done in so strange an Adventure, and not being provided for so cold a Voyage, were all frozen to death; the young Lady onely, by the light of her Beauty, the heat of her Youth, and Protection of the Gods, remaining alive: Neither was it a wonder that the men did freeze to death; for they were not onely driven to the very end or point of the Pole of that World, but even to another Pole of another World, which joined close to it; so that the cold having a double strength at the conjunction of those two Poles, was insupportable: At last, the Boat still passing on, was forced into another World; for it is impossible to round this Worlds Globe from Pole to Pole, so as we do from East to West; because the Poles of the other World, joining to the Poles of this, do not allow any further passage to surround the World that way; but if any one arrives to either of these Poles, he is either forced to return, or to enter into another World: and lest you should scruple at it, and think, if it were thus, those that live at the Poles would either see two Suns at one time, or else they would never want the Sun's light for six months together, as it is commonly believed: You must know, that each of these Worlds having its own Sun to enlighten it, they move each one in their peculiar Circles; which motion is so just and exact, that neither can hinder or obstruct the other; for they do not exceed their Tropicks: and although they should meet, yet we in this World cannot so well perceive them, by reason of the brightness of our Sun, which being nearer to us, obstructs the splendor of the Sun of the other World, they being too far off to be discerned by our optick perception, except we use very good Telescopes; by which, skilful Astronomers have often observed two or three Suns at once. But to return to the wandering Boat, and the distressed Lady; she seeing all the Men dead, found small comfort in life; their Bodies which were preserved all that while from putrefaction and stench, by the extremity of cold, began now to thaw, and corrupt; whereupon she having not strength enough to fling them over-board, was forced to remove out of her small Cabine, upon the deck, to avoid the nauseous smell; and finding the Boat swim between two plains of Ice, as a stream that runs betwixt two shores, at last perceived land, but covered all with Snow: from which came, walking upon the Ice, strange Creatures, in shape like Bears, only they went upright as men; those Creatures coming near the Boat, catched hold of it with their Paws, that served them instead of hands; some two or three of them entred first; and when they came out, the rest went in one after another; at last having viewed and observed all that was in the Boat, they spake to each other in a language which the Lady did not understand; and having carried her out of the Boat, sunk it, together with the dead men.

The Lady now finding her self in so strange a place, and amongst such wonderful kind of Creatures, was extreamly strucken with fear, and could entertain no other Thoughts, but that every moment her life was to be a sacrifice to their cruelty; but those Bear-like Creatures, how terrible soever they appear'd to her sight, yet were they so far from exercising any cruelty upon her, that rather they shewed her all civility and kindness imaginable; for she being not able to go upon the Ice, by reason of its slipperiness, they took her up in their rough arms, and carried her into their City, where instead of Houses, they had Caves under ground; and as soon as they enter'd the City, both Males and Females, young and old, flockt together to see this Lady, holding up their Paws in admiration; at last having brought her into a certain large and spacious Cave, which they intended for her reception, they left her to the custody of the Females, who entertained her with all kindness and respect, and gave her such victuals as they used to eat; but seeing her Constitution neither agreed with the temper of that Climate, nor their Diet, they were resolved to carry her into another Island of a warmer temper; in which were men like Foxes, onely walking in an upright shape, who received their neighbours the Bear-men with great civility and Courtship, very much admiring this beauteous Lady; and having discoursed some while together, agreed at last to make her a Present to the Emperor of their World; to which end, after she had made some short stay in the same place, they brought her cross that Island to a large River, whose stream run smooth and clear, like Chrystal; in which were numerous Boats, much like our Fox-traps; in one whereof she was carried, some of the Bear- and Fox-men waiting on her; and as soon as they had crossed the River, they came into an Island where there were Men which had heads, beaks and feathers, like wild-Geese, onely they went in an upright shape, like the Bear-men and Fox-men: their rumps they carried between their legs, their wings were of the same length with their Bodies, and their tails of an indifferent size, trailing after them like a Ladie's Garment; and after the Bear- and Fox-men had declared their intention and design to their Neighbours, the Geese- or Bird-men, some of them joined to the rest, and attended the Lady through that Island, till they came to another great and large River, where there was a preparation made of many Boats, much like Birds nests, onely of a bigger size; and having crost that River, they arrived into another Island, which was of a pleasant and mild temper, full of Woods and the Inhabitants thereof were Satyrs, who received both the Bear- Fox- and Bird-men, with all respect and civility; and after some conferences (for they all understood each others language) some chief of the Satyrs joining to them, accompanied the Lady out of that Island to another River, wherein were many handsome and commodious Barges; and having crost that River, they entered into a large and spacious Kingdom, the men whereof were of a Grass-Green Complexion, who entertained them very kindly, and provided all conveniences for their further voyage: hitherto they had onely crost Rivers, but now they could not avoid the open Seas any longer; wherefore they made their Ships and tacklings ready to sail over into the Island, where the Emperor of the Blazing-world (for so it was call'd) kept his residence. Very good Navigators they were; and though they had no knowledg of the Load-stone, or Needle or pendulous Watches, yet (which was as serviceable to them) they had subtile observations, and great practice; in so much that they could not onely tell the depth of the Sea in every place, but where there were shelves of Sand, Rocks, and other obstructions to be avoided by skilful and experienced Sea-men: Besides, they were excellent Augurers, which skill they counted more necessary and beneficial then the use of Compasses, Cards, Watches, and the like; but, above the rest, they had an extraordinary Art, much to be taken notice of by Experimental Philosophers, and that was a certain Engin, which would draw in a great quantity of Air, and shoot forth Wind with a great force; this Engine in a calm, they placed behind their Ships, and in a storm, before; for it served against the raging waves, like Cannons against an hostile Army, or besieged Town; it would batter and beat the waves in pieces, were they as high as Steeples; and as soon as a breach was made, they forced their passage through, in spight even of the most furious wind, using two of those Engins at every Ship, one before, to beat off the waves, and another behind to drive it on; so that the artificial wind had the better of the natural; for, it had a greater advantage of the waves, then the natural of the Ships: the natural being above the face of the Water, could not without a down right motion enter or press into the Ships; whereas the artificial with a sideward-motion, did pierce into the bowels of the Waves: Moreover, it is to be observed, that in a great Tempest they would join their Ships in battel-aray: and when they feared Wind and Waves would be too strong for them, if they divided their Ships; they joined as many together as the compass or advantage of the places of the Liquid Element would give them leave. For, their Ships were so ingeniously contrived, that they could fasten them together as close as a Honey-comb, without waste of place; and being thus united, no Wind nor Waves were able to separate them. The Emperor's Ships, were all of Gold; but the Merchants and Skippers, of Leather; the Golden Ships were not much heavier then ours of Wood, by reason they were neatly made, and required not such thickness, neither were they troubled with Pitch, Tar, Pumps, Guns, and the like, which make our Woodden-Ships very heavy; for though they were not all of a piece, yet they were so well sodder'd, that there was no fear of Leaks, Chinks, or Clefts; and as for Guns, there was no use of them, because they had no other enemies but the Winds: But the Leather Ships were not altogether so sure, although much leighter; besides, they were pitched to keep out Water.

Having thus prepar'd, and order'd their Navy, they went on in despight of Calm or Storm: And though the Lady at first fancied her self in a very sad condition, and her mind was much tormented with doubts and fears, not knowing whether this strange Adventure would tend to her safety or destruction; yet she being withal of a generous spirit, and ready wit, considering what dangers she had past, and finding those sorts of men civil and diligent attendants to her, took courage, and endeavoured to learn their language; which after she had obtained so far, that partly by some words and signs she was able to apprehend their meaning, she was so far from being afraid of them, that she thought her self not onely safe, but very happy in their company: By which we may see, that Novelty discomposes the mind, but acquaintance settles it in peace and tranquillity. At last, having passed by several rich Islands and Kingdoms, they went towards Paradise, which was the seat of the Emperor; and coming in sight of it, rejoiced very much; the Lady at first could perceive nothing but high Rocks, which seemed to touch the Skies; and although they appear'd not of an equal heigth, yet they seemed to be all one piece, without partitions: but at last drawing nearer, she perceived a clift, which was a part of those Rocks, out of which she spied coming forth a great number of Boats, which afar off shewed like a company of Ants, marching one after another; the Boats appeared like the holes or partitions in a Honey-comb, and when joined together, stood as close; the men were of several Complexions, but none like any of our World; and when both the Boats and Ships met, they saluted and spake to each other very courteously; for there was but one language in all that World: nor no more but one Emperor, to whom they all submitted with the greatest duty and obedience, which made them live in a continued Peace and Happiness; not acquainted with Foreign Wars or Home-bred Insurrections. The Lady now being arrived at this place, was carried out of her Ship into one of those Boats, and conveighed through the same passage (for there was no other) into that part of the World where the Emperor did reside; which part was very pleasant, and of a mild temper: Within it self it was divided by a great number of vast and large Rivers, all ebbing and flowing, into several Islands of unequal distance from each other, which in most parts were as pleasant, healthful, rich, and fruitful, as Nature could make them; and, as I mentioned before, secure from all Foreign Invasions, by reason there was but one way to enter, and that like a Labyrinth, so winding and turning among the Rocks, that no other Vessels but small Boats, could pass, carrying not above three passengers at a time: On each side all along the narrow and winding River, there were several Cities, some of Marble, some of Alabaster, some of Agat, some of Amber, some of Coral, and some of other precious materials not known in our world; all which after the Lady had passed, she came to the Imperial City, named Paradise, which appeared in form like several Islands; for, Rivers did run betwixt every street, which together with the Bridges, whereof there was a great number, were all paved. The City it self was built of Gold; and their Architectures were noble, stately, and magnificent, not like our Modern, but like those in the Romans time; for, our Modern Buildings are like those Houses which Children use to make of Cards, one story above another, fitter for Birds, then Men; but theirs were more Large, and Broad, then high; the highest of them did not exceed two stories, besides those rooms that were under-ground, as Cellars, and other Offices. The Emperor's Palace stood upon an indifferent ascent from the Imperial City; at the top of which ascent was a broad Arch, supported by several Pillars, which went round the Palace, and contained four of our English miles in compass: within the Arch stood the Emperor's Guard, which consisted of several sorts of Men; at every half mile, was a Gate to enter, and every Gate was of a different fashion; the first, which allowed a passage from the Imperial City into the Palace, had on either hand a Cloyster, the outward part whereof stood upon Arches sustained by Pillars, but the inner part was close: Being entred through the Gate, the Palace it self appear'd in its middle like the Isle of a Church, a mile and a half long, and half a mile broad; the roof of it was all Arched, and rested upon Pillars, so artificially placed that a stranger would lose himself therein without a Guide; at the extream sides, that is, between the outward and inward part of the Cloyster, were Lodgings for Attendants; and in the midst of the Palace, the Emperor's own Rooms; whose Lights were placed at the top of every one, because of the heat of the Sun: the Emperor's appartment for State was no more inclosed then the rest; onely an Imperial Throne was in every appartment, of which the several adornments could not be perceived until one entered, because the Pillars were so just opposite to one another, that all the adornments could not be seen at one. The first part of the Palace was, as the Imperial City, all of Gold; and when it came to the Emperors appartment, it was so rich with Diamonds, Pearls, Rubies, and the like precious Stones, that it surpasses my skill to enumerate them all. Amongst the rest, the Imperial Room of State appear'd most magnificent; it was paved with green Diamonds (for there are in that World Diamonds of all Colours) so artificially, as it seemed but of one piece; the Pillars were set with Diamonds so close, and in such a manner, that they appear'd most Glorious to the sight; between every Pillar was a Bow or Arch of a certain sort of Diamonds, the like whereof our World does not afford; which being placed in every one of the Arches in several rows, seemed just like so many Rainbows of several different colours. The roof of the Arches was of blew Diamonds, and in the midst thereof was a Carbuncle, which represented the Sun; and the Rising and Setting-Sun at the East and West-side of the Room were made of Rubies. Out of this Room there was a passage into the Emperor's Bed-Chamber, the Walls whereof were of Jet, and the Floor of black Marble; the Roof was of Mother of Pearl, where the Moon and Blazing-Stars were represented by white Diamonds, and his Bed was made of Diamonds and Carbuncles.

    No sooner was the Lady brought before the Emperor, but he conceived her to be some Goddess, and offered to worship her; which she refused, telling him, (for by that time she had pretty well learned their Language) that although she came out of another world, yet was she but a mortal. At which the Emperor rejoycing, made her his Wife, and gave her an absolute power to rule and govern all that World as she pleased. But her subjects, who could hardly be perswaded to believe her mortal, tender'd her all the Veneration and Worship due to a Deity.

    Her Accoustrement after she was made Empress, was as followeth: On her head she wore a Cap of Pearl, and a Half-moon of Diamonds just before it; on the top of her Crown came spreading over a broad Carbuncle, cut in the form of the Sun; her Coat was of Pearl, mixt with blew

Diamonds, and frindged with red ones; her Buskins and Sandals were of green Diamonds; In her left hand she held a Buckler, to signifie the Defence of her Dominions; which Buckler was made of that sort of Diamond as has several different Colours; and being cut and made in the form of an Arch, shewed like a Rain-bow; In her right hand she carried a Spear made of white Diamond, cut like the tail of a Blazing Star, which signified that she was ready to assault those that proved her Enemies.

None was allowed to use or wear Gold but those of the Imperial Race, which were the onely Nobles of the State; nor durst any one wear Jewels but the Emperor, the Empress and their Eldest Son; notwithstanding that they had an infinite quantity both of Gold and precious Stones in that World; for they had larger extents of Gold, then our Arabian Sands; their precious Stones were Rocks, and their Diamonds of several Colours; they used no Coyn, but all their Traffick was by exchange of several Commodities.

Their Priests and Governors were Princes of the Imperial Blood, and made Eunuches for that purpose; and as for the ordinary sort of men in that part of the World where the Emperor resided, they were of several Complexions; not white, black, tawny, olive or ash-coloured; but some appear'd of an Azure, some of a deep Purple, some of a Grass-green, some of a Scarlet, some of an Orange-colour, &c. Which Colours and Complexions, whether they were made by the bare reflection of light, without the assistance of small particles; or by the help of well-ranged and order'd Atoms; or by a continual agitation of little Globules; or by some pressing and re-acting motion, I am not able to determine. The rest of the Inhabitants of that World, were men of several different sorts, shapes, figures, dispositions, and humors, as I have already made mention, heretofore; some were Bear-men, some Worm-men, some Fish- or Mear-men, otherwise called Syrens; some Bird-men, some Fly-men, some Ant-men, some Geese-men, some Spider-men, some Lice-men, some Fox-men, some Ape-men, some Jack daw-men, some Magpie-men, some Parrot-men, some Satyrs, some Gyants, and many more, which I cannot all remember; and of these several sorts of men, each followed such a profession as was most proper for the nature of their Species, which the Empress encouraged them in, especially those that had applied themselves to the study of several Arts and Sciences; for they were as ingenious and witty in the invention of profitable and useful Arts, as we are in our world, nay, more; and to that end she erected Schools, and founded several Societies. The Bear-men were to be her Experimental Philosophers, the Bird-men her Astronomers, the Fly- Worm- and Fish-men her Natural Philosophers, the Ape-men her Chymists, the Satyrs her Galenick Physicians, the Fox-men her Politicians, the Spider- and Lice-men her Mathematicians, the Jackdaw- Magpie- and Parrot-men her Orators and Logicians, the Gyants her Architects, &c. But before all things, she having got a Soveraign power from the Emperor over all the World, desired to be informed both of the manner of their Religion and Government; and to that end she called the Priests and States men, to give her an account of either. Of the States men she enquired, first, Why they had so few Laws? To which they answered, That many Laws made many Divisions, which most commonly did breed Factions, and at last brake out into open Wars. Next, she asked, Why they preferred the Monarchical form of Government before any other? They answered, That as it was natural for one Body to have but one Head, so it was also natural for a Politick body to have but one Governor; and that a Common-wealth, which had many Governors was like a Monster with many Heads. Besides, said they, a Monarchy is a divine form of Government, and agrees most with our Religion: For as there is but one God, whom we all unanimously worship and adore with one Faith; so we are resolved to have but one Emperor, to whom we all submit with one obedience.

Then the Empress seeing that the several sorts of her Subjects had each their Churches apart, asked the Priests, whether they were of several Religions? They answered her Majesty, That there was no more but one Religion in all that World, nor no diversity of opinions in that same Religion for though there were several sorts of men, yet had they all but one opinion concerning the Worship and Adoration of God. The Empress asked them, Whether they were Jews, Turks, or Christians? We do not know, said they, what Religions those are; but we do all unanimously acknowledg, worship and adore the Onely, Omnipotent, and Eternal God, with all reverence, submission, and duty. Again, the Empress enquired, Whether they had several Forms of Worship? They answered, No: For our Devotion and Worship consists onely in Prayers, which we frame according to our several Necessities, in Petitions, Humiliations, Thanksgiving, &c. Truly, replied the Empress, I thought you had been either Jews, or Turks, because I never perceived any Women in your

Congregations: But what is the reason, you bar them from your religious Assemblies? It is not fit, said they, that Men and Women should be promiscuously together in time of Religious Worship; for their company hinders Devotion, and makes many, instead of praying to God, direct their Devotion to their Mistresses. But, asked the Empress, Have they no Congregation of their own, to perform the duties of Divine Worship, as well as Men? No, answered they: but they stay at home, and say their Prayers by themselves in their Closets. Then the Empress desir'd to know the reason why the Priests and Governors of their World were made Eunuchs? They answer'd, To keep them from Marriage: For Women and Children most commonly make disturbance both in Church and State. But, said she, Women and Children have no Employment in Church or State. 'Tis true, answer'd they; but, although they are not admitted to publick Employments, yet are they so prevalent with their Husbands and Parents, that many times by their importunate perswasions, they cause as much, nay, more mischief secretly, then if they had the management of publick Affairs.

The Empress having received an information of what concerned both Church and State, passed some time in viewing the Imperial Palace, where she admired much the skil and ingenuity of the Architects, and enquired of them, first, Why they built their Houses no higher then two stories from the Ground? They answered her Majesty, That the lower their Buildings were, the less were they subject either to the heat of the Sun, or Wind, Tempest, Decay, &c. Then she desired to know the reason, why they made them so thick? They answered, That, the thicker the Walls were, the warmer they were in Winter, the cooler in Summer; for their thickness kept out both the Cold and Heat. Lastly, she asked, Why they Arched their Roofs, and made so many Pillars? They replied, That Arches and Pillars, did not onely grace a Building very much, and caused it to appear Magnificent, but made it also firm and lasting.

The Empress was very well satisfied with their answers; and after some time, when she thought that her new founded societies of the Vertuoso's had made a good progress in the several Employments she had put them upon, she caused a Convocation first of the Bird-men, and commanded them to give her a true relation of the two Cœlestial Bodies, viz. the Sun and Moon, which they did with all the obedience and faithfulness befitting their duty.

The Sun, as much as they could observe, they related to be a firm or solid Stone, of a vast bigness; of colour yellowish, and of an extraordinary splendor: But the Moon, they said, was of a whitish colour; and although she looked dim in the presence of the Sun, yet had she her own light, and was a shining body of her self, as might be perceived by her vigorous appearance in Moon-shiny-nights; the difference onely betwixt her own and the Sun's light was, that the Sun did strike his beams in a direct line; but the Moon never respected the Centre of their World in a right line, but her Centre was always excentrical. The Spots both in the Sun and Moon, as far as they were able to perceive, they affirmed to be nothing else but flaws and stains of their stony Bodies. Concerning the heat of the Sun, they were not of one opinion; some would have the Sun hot in it self, alledging an old Tradition, that it should at some time break asunder, and burn the Heavens, and consume this world into hot Embers, which, said they, could not be done, if the Sun were not fiery of it self. Others again said, This opinion could not stand with reason; for Fire being a destroyer of all things, the Sun-Stone after this manner would burn up all the near adjoining Bodies: Besides, said they, Fire cannot subsist without fuel; and the Sun-Stone having nothing to feed on, would in a short time consume it self; wherefore they thought it more probable that the Sun was not actually hot, but onely by the reflection of its light; so that its heat was an effect of its light, both being immaterial. But this opinion again was laught at by others, and rejected as ridiculous, who thought it impossible that one immaterial should produce another; and believed that both the light and heat of the Sun proceeded from a swift Circular motion of the Æthereal Globules, which by their striking upon the Optick nerve, caused light, and their motion produced heat: But neither would this opinion hold; for, said some, then it would follow, that the sight of Animals is the cause of light; and that, were there no eyes, there would be no light; which was against all sense and reason. Thus they argued concerning the heat and light of the Sun; but, which is remarkable, none did say, that the Sun was a Globous fluid body, and had a swift Circular motion; but all agreed, It was fixt and firm like a Center, and therefore they generally called it the Sun-Stone.

Then the Empress asked them the reason, Why the Sun and Moon did often appear in different postures or shapes, as sometimes magnified, sometimes diminished; sometimes elevated, otherwhiles depressed; now thrown to the right, and then to the left? To which some of the Bird-men answered, That it proceeded from the various degrees of heat and cold, which are found in the Air, from whence did follow a differing density and rarity; and likewise from the vapours that are interposed, whereof those that ascend are higher and less dense then the ambient air, but those which descend are heavier and more dense. But others did with more probability affirm, that it was nothing else but the various patterns of the Air; for like as Painters do not copy out one and the same original just alike at all times; so, said they, do several parts of the Air make different patterns of the luminous Bodies of the Sun and Moon: which patterns, as several copies, the sensitive motions do figure out in the substance of our eyes.

This answer the Empress liked much better then the former, and enquired further, What opinion they had of those Creatures that are called the motes of the Sun? To which they answered, That they were nothing else but streams of very small, rare and transparent particles, through which the Sun was represented as through a glass: for if they were not transparent, said they, they would eclipse the light of the Sun; and if not rare and of an airy substance, they would hinder Flies from flying in the Air, at least retard their flying motion: Nevertheless, although they were thinner then the thinnest vapour, yet were they not so thin as the body of air, or else they would not be perceptible by animal sight. Then the Empress asked, Whether they were living Creatures? They answered, Yes: Because they did encrease and decrease, and were nourished by the presence, and starved by the absence of the Sun.

Having thus finished their discourse of the Sun and Moon, the Empress desired to know what Stars there were besides? But they answer'd, that they could perceive in that World none other but Blazing Stars, and from thence it had the name that it was called the Blazing-World; and these Blazing-Stars, said they, were such solid, firm and shining bodies as the Sun and Moon, not of a Globular, but of several sorts of figures: some had tails; and some, other kinds of shapes.

After this, The Empress asked them, What kind of substance or creature the Air was? The Bird-men answered, That they could have no other perception of the Air, but by their own Respiration: For, said they, some bodies are onely subject to touch, others onely to sight, and others onely to smell; but some are subject to none of our exterior Senses: For Nature is so full of variety, that our weak Senses cannot perceive all the various sorts of her Creatures; neither is there any one object perceptible by all our Senses, no more then several objects are by one sense. I believe you, replied the Empress; but if you can give no account of the Air, said she, you will hardly be able to inform me how Wind is made; for they say, that Wind is nothing but motion of the Air. The Bird-men answer'd, That they observed Wind to be more dense then Air, and therefore subject to the sense of Touch; but what properly Wind was, and the manner how it was made, they could not exactly tell; some said, it was caused by the Clouds falling on each other; and others, that it was produced of a hot and dry exhalation: which ascending, was driven down again by the coldness of the Air that is in the middle Region, and by reason of its leightness, could not go directly to the bottom, but was carried by the Air up and down: Some would have it a flowing Water of the Air; and others again, a flowing Air moved by the blaz of the Stars.

But the Empress, seeing they could not agree concerning the cause of Wind, asked, Whether they could tell how Snow was made? To which they answered That according to their observation, Snow was made by a commixture of Water, and some certain extract of the Element of Fire that is under the Moon; a small portion of which extract, being mixed with Water, and beaten by Air or Wind, made a white Froth called Snow; which being after some while dissolved by the heat of the same spirit, turned to Water again. This observation amazed the Empress very much; for she had hitherto believed, That Snow was made by cold motions, and not by such an agitation or beating of a fiery extract upon water: Nor could she be perswaded to believe it until the Fish- or Mear-men had delivered their observation upon the making of Ice, which, they said, was not produced, as some hitherto conceived, by the motion of the Air, raking the Superficies of the Earth, but by some strong saline vapour arising out of the Seas, which condensed Water into Ice; and the more quantity there was of that vapour, the greater were the Mountains of Precipices of Ice; but the reason that it did not so much freeze in the Torrid Zone, or under the Ecliptick, as near or under the Poles, was, that this vapour in those places being drawn up by the Sun-beams into the middle Region of the Air, was onely condensed into Water, and fell down in showres of Rain; when as, under the Poles, the heat of the Sun being not so vehement, the same vapour had no force or power to rise so high, and therefore caused so much Ice, by ascending and acting onely upon the surface of water.

This Relation confirmed partly the observation of the Bird-men concerning the cause of Snow; but since they had made mention that that same extract, which by its commixture with Water made Snow, proceeded from the Element of Fire, that is under the Moon: The Emperess asked them, of what nature that Elementary Fire was; whether it was like ordinary Fire here upon Earth, or such a Fire as is within the bowels of the Earth, and as the famous Mountains Vesuvius and Ætna do burn withal; or whether it was such a sort of fire, as is found in flints, &c. They answered, That the Elementary Fire, which is underneath the Sun, was not so solid as any of those mentioned fires; because it had no solid fuel to feed on; but yet it was much like the flame of ordinary fire, onely somewhat more thin and fluid; for Flame, said they, is nothing else but the airy part of a fired Body.

Lastly, the Empress asked the Bird-men of the nature of Thunder and Lightning? and whether it was not caused by roves of Ice falling upon each other? To which they answered, That it was not made that way, but by an encounter of cold and heat; so that an exhalation being kindled in the Clouds, did dash forth Lightning, and that there were so many rentings of Clouds as there were Sounds and Cracking noises: But this opinion was contradicted by others, who affirmed that Thunder was a sudden and monstrous Blaz, stirred up in the Air, and did not always require a Cloud; but the Empress not knowing what they meant by Blaz (for even they themselves were not able to explain the sense of this word) liked the former better; and, to avoid hereafter tedious disputes, and have the truth of the Phænomena's of Cœlestial Bodies more exactly known, commanded the Bear-men, which were her Experimental Philosophers, to observe them through such Instruments as are called Telescopes, which they did according to her Majesties Command; but these Telescopes caused more differences and divisions amongst them, then ever they had before; for some said, they perceived that the Sun stood still, and the Earth did move about it; others were of opinion, that they both did move; and others said again, that the Earth stood still, and Sun did move; some counted more Stars then others; some discovered new Stars never seen before; some fell into a great dispute with others concerning the bigness of the Stars; some said, The Moon was another World like their Terrestrial Globe, and the spots therein were Hills and Vallies; but others would have the spots to be the Terrestrial parts, and the smooth and glossie parts, the

Sea: At last, the Empress commanded them to go with their Telescopes to the very end of the Pole that was joined to the World she came from, and try whether they could perceive any Stars in it: which they did; and, being returned to her Majesty, reported that they had seen three Blazing-Stars appear there, one after another in a short time, whereof two were bright, and one dim; but they could not agree neither in this observation: for some said, It was but one Star which appeared at three several times, in several places; and others would have them to be three several Stars; for they thought it impossible, that those three several appearances should have been but one Star, because every Star did rise at a certain time, and appear'd in a certain place, and did disappear in the same place: Next, It is altogether improbable, said they, That one Star should fly from place to place, especially at such a vast distance, without a visible motion; in so short a time, and appear in such different places, whereof two were quite opposite, and the third side-ways: Lastly, If it had been but one Star, said they, it would always have kept the same splendor, which it did not; for, as above mentioned, two were bright, and one was dim. After they had thus argued, the Empress began to grow angry at their Telescopes, that they could give no better Intelligence; for, said she, now I do plainly perceive, that your Glasses are false Informers, and instead of discovering the Truth, delude your Senses; Wherefore I Command you to break them, and let the Bird-men trust onely to their natural eyes, and examine Cœlestial Objects by the motions of their own Sense and Reason. The Bear-men replied, That it was not the fault of their Glasses, which caused such differences in their Opinions, but the sensitive motions in their Optick organs did not move alike, nor were their rational judgments always regular: To which the Empress answered, That if their Glasses were true Informers, they would rectifie their irregular Sense and Reason; But, said she, Nature has made your Sense and Reason more regular then Art has your Glasses; for they are meer deluders, and will never lead you to the knowledg of Truth; Wherefore I command you again to break them; for you may observe the progressive motions of Cœlestial Bodies with your natural eyes better then through Artificial Glasses. The Bear-men being exceedingly troubled at her Majesties displeasure concerning their Telescopes, kneel'd down, and in the humblest manner petitioned, that they might not be broken; for, said they, we take more delight in Artificial delusions, then in Natural truths. Besides, we shall want Imployments for our Senses, and Subjects for Arguments; for, were there nothing but truth, and no falshood, there would be no occasion to dispute, and by this means we should want the aim and pleasure of our endeavors in confuting and contradicting each other; neither would one man be thought wiser then another, but all would either be alike knowing and wise, or all would be fools; wherefore we most humbly beseech your Imperial Majesty to spare our Glasses, which are our onely delight, and as dear to us as our lives. The Empress at last consented to their request, but upon condition, that their disputes and quarrels should remain within their Schools, and cause no factions or disturbances in State, or Government. The Bear-men, full of joy, returned their most humble thanks to the Empress; and to make her amends for the displeasure which their Telescopes had occasioned, told her Majesty, that they had several other artificial Optick-Glasses, which they were sure would give her Majesty a great deal more satisfaction. Amongst the rest, they brought forth several Microscopes, by the means of which they could enlarge the shapes of little bodies, and make a Lowse appear as big as an Elephant, and a Mite as big as a Whale. First of all they shewed the Empress a gray Drone-flye, wherein they observed that the greatest part of her face, nay, of her head, consisted of two large bunches all cover'd over with a multitude of small Pearls or Hemispheres in a Trigonal order: Which Pearls were of two degrees, smaller and bigger; the smaller degree was lowermost, and looked towards the ground; the other was upward, and looked sideward, forward and backward: They were all so smooth and polished, that they were able to represent the image of any object, the number of them was in all 14000. After the view of this strange and miraculous Creature, and their several observations upon it, the Empress asked them, What they judged those little Hemispheres might be? They answered, That each of them was a perfect Eye, by reason they perceived that each was covered with a Transparent Cornea, containing a liquor within them, which resembled the watery or glassie humor of the Eye. To which the Emperess replied, That they might be glassie Pearls, and yet not Eyes; and that perhaps their Microscopes did not truly inform them. But they smilingly answered her Majesty, That she did not know the vertue of those Microscopes: for they never delude, but rectifie and inform the Senses; nay, the World, said they, would be but blind without them, as it has been in former ages before those Microscopes were invented.

After this, they took a Charcoal, and viewing it with one of their best Microscopes, discovered in it an infinite multitude of pores, some bigger, some less; so close and thick, that they left but very little space betwixt them to be filled with a solid body; and to give her Imperial Majesty a better assurance thereof, they counted in a line of them an inch long, no less then 2700 pores; from which Observation they drew this following Conclusion, to wit, That this multitude of pores was the cause of the blackness of the Coal; for, said they, a body that has so many pores, from each of which no light is reflected, must necessarily look black, since black is nothing else but a privation of light, or a want of reflection. But the Empress replied, That if all Colours were made by reflection of light, and that Black was as much a colour as any other colour; then certainly they contradicted themselves in saying that black was made by want of reflection. However, not to interrupt your Microscopical Inspections, said she, let us see how Vegetables appear through your Glasses; whereupon they took a Nettle, and by the vertue of the Microscope, discovered that underneath the points of the Nettle there were certain little bags or bladders, containing a poysonous liquor, and when the points had made way into the interior parts of the skin, they like Syringe-pipes served to conveigh that same liquor into them. To which Observation the Empress replied, That if there were such poyson in Nettles, then certainly in eating of them, they would hurt us inwardly, as much as they do outwardly? But they answered, That it belonged to Physicians more then to Experimental Philosophers, to give Reasons hereof; for they only made Microscopical inspections, and related the Figures of the Natural parts of Creatures according to the representation of their glasses.

Lastly, They shewed the Empress a Flea, and a Lowse; which Creatures through the Microscope appear'd so terrible to her sight, that they had almost put her into a swoon; the description of all their parts would be very tedious to relate, and therefore I'le forbear it at this present. The Empress, after the view of those strangely-shaped Creatures, pitied much those that are molested with them, especially poor Beggars, which although they have nothing to live on themselves, are yet necessitated to maintain and feed of their own flesh and blood, a company of such terrible Creatures called Lice; who, instead of thanks, do reward them with pains, and torment them for giving them nourishment and food. But after the Empress had seen the shapes of these monstrous Creatures, she desir'd to know, Whether their Microscopes could hinder their biting, or at least shew some means how to avoid them? To which they answered, That such Arts were mechanical and below the noble study of Microscopical observations. Then the Empress asked them, Whether they had not such sorts of Glasses that could enlarge and magnifie the shapes of great Bodies as well as they had done of little ones? Whereupon they took one of their best and largest Microscopes, and endeavoured to view a Whale thorow it; but alas! the shape of the Whale was so big, that its Circumference went beyond the magnifying quality of the Glass; whether the error proceeded from the Glass, or from a wrong position of the Whale against the reflection of light, I cannot certainly tell. The Empress seeing the insufficiency of those Magnifying-Glasses, that they were not able to enlarge all sorts of Objects, asked the Bear-men, whether they could not make Glasses of a contrary nature to those they had shewed her, to wit, such as instead of enlarging or magnifying the shape or figure of an Object, could contract it beneath its natural proportion: Which, in obedience to her Majesties Commands, they did; and viewing through one of the best of them, a huge and mighty Whale appear'd no bigger then a Sprat; nay, through some no bigger then a Vinegar-Eele; and through their ordinary ones, an Elephant seemed no bigger then a Flea; a Camel no bigger then a Lowse; and an Ostrich no bigger then a Mite. To relate all their Optick observations through the several sorts of their Glasses, would be a tedious work, and tire even the most patient Reader, wherefore I'le pass them by; onely this was very remarkable and worthy to be taken notice of, that notwithstanding their great skil, industry and ingenuity in Experimental Philosophy, they could yet by no means contrive such Glasses, by the help of which they could spy out a Vacuum, with all its dimensions, nor Immaterial substances, Non-beings, and Mixt-beings, or such as are between something and nothing; which they were very much troubled at, hoping that yet, in time, by long study and practice, they might perhaps attain to it.

  The Bird- and Bear-men being dismissed, the Empress called both the Syrens- or Fish-men, and the Worm-men, to deliver their Observations which they had made, both within the Seas, and the Earth. First, she enquired of the Fish-men whence the saltness of the Sea did proceed? To which they answered, That there was a volatile salt in those parts of the Earth, which as a bosom contain the Waters of the Sea, which Salt being imbibed by the Sea, became fixt; and this imbibing motion was that they call'd the Ebbing and Flowing of the Sea; for, said they, the rising and swelling of the Water, is caused by those parts of the volatile Salt as are not so easily imbibed, which striving to ascend above the Water, bear it up with such a motion, as Man, or some other Animal Creature, in a violent exercise uses to take breath. This they affirmed to be the true cause both of the saltness, and the ebbing and flowing-motion of the Sea, and not the jogging of the Earth, or the secret influence of the Moon, as some others had made the World believe.

After this, the Empress enquired, Whether they had observed, that all Animal Creatures within the Seas and other waters, had blood? They answered, That some had blood, more or less, but some had none. In Crea-fishes and Lobsters, said they, we perceive but little blood; but in Crabs, Oysters, Cockles, &c. none at all. Then the Empress asked them, in what part of their Bodies that little blood did reside? They answered, in a small vein, which in Lobsters went through the middle of their tails, but in Crea-fishes was found in their backs: as for other sorts of Fishes, some, said they, had onely blood about their Gills, and others in some other places of their Bodies; but they had not as yet observed any whose veins did spread all over their Bodies. The Empress wondring that there could be living Animals without Blood, to be better satisfied, desired the Worm-men to inform her, whether they had observed Blood in all sorts of Worms? They answered, That, as much as they could perceive, some had Blood, and some not; a Moth, said they, had no Blood at all, and a Lowse had, but like a Lobster, a little Vein along her back: Also Nits, Snails, and Maggots, as well as those that are generated out of Cheese and Fruits, as those that are produced out of Flesh, had no blood: But, replied the Empress, If those mentioned creatures have no blood, how is it possible they can live? for it is commonly said, That the life of an Animal consists in the blood, which is the seat of the Animal spirits. They answered, That blood was not a necessary propriety to the life of an Animal; and that that which was commonly called Animal spirits, was nothing else but corporeal motions proper to the nature and figure of an Animal. Then she asked both the Fish- and Worm-men, whether all those Creatures that have blood, had a circulation of blood in their veins and arteries? But they answered, That it was impossible to give her Majesty an exact account thereof, by reason the circulation of blood was an interior motion, which their senses, neither of themselves, nor by the help of any Optick Instrument could perceive; but as soon as they had dissected an Animal Creature, to find out the truth thereof, the interior corporeal motions proper to that particular figure or creature, were altered. Then said the Empress, If all Animal Creatures have not blood, it is certain, they all have neither Muscles, tendons, nerves, &c. But, said she, Have you ever observed Animal Creatures that are neither flesh, nor Fish, but of an intermediate degree between both? Truly, answered both the Fish- and Worm-men, We have observed several Animal Creatures that live both in Water, and on the Earth, indifferently, and if any, certainly those may be said to be of such a mixt nature, that is, partly Flesh, and partly Fish: But how is it possible, replied the Empress, that they should live both in Water, and on the Earth, since those Animals that live by the respiration of Air, cannot live within Water; and those that live in Water, cannot live by the respiration of Air, as Experience doth sufficiently witness. They answered her Majesty, That as there were different sorts of Creatures, so they had also different ways of Respirations; for Respiration, said they, is nothing else but a composition and division of parts, and the motions of nature being infinitely various, it is impossible that all Creatures should have the like motions; wherefore it was not necessary, that all Animal Creatures should be bound to live either by the Air, or by Water onely, but according as Nature had ordered it convenient to their Species. The Empress seem'd very well satisfied with their answer, and desired to be further informed, Whether all Animal Creatures did continue their Species by a successive propogation of particulars, and whether in every Species the off-springs did always resemble their Generator or Producer, both in their interior and exterior Figures? They answered, her Majesty, That some Species or sorts of Creatures, were kept up by a successive propagation of an off-spring that was like the producer, but some were not. Of the first rank, said they, are all those Animals that are of different sexes, besides several others; but of the second rank are for the most part those we call Insects, whose production proceds from such causes as have no conformity or likeness with their produced Effects; as for example, Maggots bred out of Cheese, and several others generated out of Earth, Water, and the like. But said the Empress, there is some likeness between Maggots and Cheese; for Cheese has no blood, nor Maggots neither; besides, they have almost the same taste which Cheese has. This proves nothing, answered they; for Maggots have a visible, local, progressive motion, which Cheese hath not. The Empress replied, That when all the Cheese was turned into Maggots, it might be said to have local, progressive motion. They answered, That when the Cheese by its own figurative motions was changed into Maggots, it was no more Cheese. The Empress confessed that she observed Nature was infinitely various in her works, and that though the species of Creatures did continue, yet their particulars were subject to infinite changes. But since you have informed me, said she, of the various sorts and productions of Animal Creatures, I desire you to tell me what you have observed of their sensitive perceptions? Truly, answered they, Your Majesty puts a very hard question to us, and we shall hardly be able to give a satisfactory answer to it; for there are many different sorts of Creatures, which as they have all different perceptions, so they have also different organs, which our senses are not able to discover, onely in an Oystershell we have with admiration observed, that the common sensorium of the Oyster lies just as the closing of the shells, where the pressure and re-action may be perceived by the opening and shutting of the shells every tide.

After all this, the Empress desired the Worm men to give her a true Relation how frost was made upon the Earth? To which they answered, That it was made much after the manner and description of the Fish- and Bird-men, concerning the Congelation of Water into Ice and Snow, by a commixture of saline and acid particles; which relation added a great light to the Ape-men, who were the Chymists, concerning their Chymical principles, Salt, Sulphur, and Mercury. But, said the Empress, if it be so, it will require an infinite multitude of saline particles to produce such a great quantity of Ice, Frost and Snow: besides, said she, when Snow, Ice and Frost, turn again into their former principle, I would fain know what becomes of those saline particles? But neither the Worm-men, nor the Fish- and Bird-men, could give her an answer to it.

Then the Empress enquired of them the reason, Why Springs were not as salt as the Sea is? also, why some did ebb and flow? To which it was answered, That the ebbing and flowing of some Springs, was caused by hollow Caverns within the Earth, where the Seawater crowding thorow, did thrust forward, and drew backward the Spring-water, according to its own way of ebbing and flowing; but others said, That it proceeded from a small proportion of saline and acid particles, which the Spring-water imbibed from the Earth; and although it was not so much as to be perceived by the sense of Taste; yet it was enough to cause an ebbing and flowing-motion. And as for the Spring-water being fresh, they gave, according to their Observation, this following reason: There is, said they, a certain heat within the Bowels of the Earth, proceeding from its swift circular motion, upon its own axe, which heat distills the rarest parts of the Earth into a fresh and insipid water, which water being through the pores of the Earth, conveighed into a place where it may break forth without resistance or obstruction, causes Springs and Fountains; and these distilled Waters within the Earth, do nourish and refresh the grosser and drier parts thereof. This Relation confirmed the Empress in the opinion concerning the motion of the Earth, and the fixedness of the Sun, as the Bird-men had informed her; and then she asked the Worm-men, whether Minerals and Vegetables were generated by the same heat that is within the Bowels of the Earth? To which they could give her no positive answer; onely this they affirmed, That heat and cold were not the primary producing causes of either Vegetables or Minerals, or other sorts of Creatures, but onely effects; and to prove this our assertion, said they, we have observed, that by change of some sorts of Corporeal motions, that which is now hot, will become cold; and what is now cold, will grow hot; but the hottest place of all, we find to be the Center of the Earth: Neither do we observe, that the Torrid Zone does contain so much Gold and Silver as the Temperate; nor is there great store of Iron and Lead wheresoever there is Gold; for these Metals are most found in colder Climates towards either of the Poles. This Observation, the Empress commanded them to confer with her Chymists, the Ape-men; to let them know that Gold was not produced by a violent, but a temperate degree of heat. She asked further, Whether Gold could not be made by Art? They answered, That they could not certainly tell her Majesty, but if it was possible to be done, they thought Tin, Lead, Brass, Iron and Silver, to be the fittest Metals for such an Artificial Transmutation. Then she asked them, Whether Art could produce Iron, Tin, Lead, or Silver? They answered, Not, in their opinion. Then I perceive, replyed the Empress, that your judgments are very irregular, since you believe that Gold, which is so fixt a Metal, that nothing has been found as yet which could occasion a dissolution of its interior figure, may be made by Art, and not Tin, Lead, Iron, Copper or Silver, which yet are so far weaker, and meaner Metals then Gold is. But the Worm-men excused themselves, that they were ignorant in that Art, and that such questions belonged more properly to the Ape-men, which were Her Majesties Chymists.

Then the Empress asked them, Whether by their Sensitive perceptions they could observe the interior corporeal, figurative Motions both of Vegetables and Minerals? They answer'd, That their Senses could perceive them after they were produced, but not before; Nevertheless, said they, although the interior, figurative motions of Natural Creatures are not subject to the exterior, animal, sensitive perceptions, yet by their Rational perception they may judg of them, and of their productions if they be regular: Whereupon the Empress commanded the Bear-men to lend them some of their best Microscopes. At which the Bear-men smilingly answered her Majesty, that their Glasses would do them but little service in the bowels of the Earth, because there was no light; for, said they, our Glasses do onely represent exterior objects, according to the various reflections and positions of light; and wheresoever light is wanting, the glasses wil do no good. To which the Worm-men replied, that although they could not say much of refractions, reflections, inflections, and the like; yet were they not blind, even in the bowels of the Earth: for they could see the several sorts of Minerals, as also minute Animals, that lived there; which minute Animal Creatures were not blind neither, but had some kind of sensitive perception that was as serviceable to them, as sight, taste, smell, touch, hearing, &c. was to other Animal Creatures: By which it is evident, That Nature has been as bountiful to those Creatures that live underground, or in the bowels of the Earth, as to those that live upon the surface of the Earth, or in the Air, or in Water. But howsoever, proceeded the Worm-men, although there is light in the bowels of the Earth, yet your Microscopes will do but little good there, by reason those Creatures that live under ground have not such an optick sense as those that live on the surface of the Earth: wherefore, unless you had such Glasses as are proper for their perception, your Microscopes will not be any ways advantagious to them. The Empress seem'd well pleased with this answer of the Worm-men; and asked them further, Whether Minerals and all other Creatures within the Earth were colourless? At which question they could not forbear laughing; and when the Empress asked the reason why they laught? We most humbly beg your Majesties pardon, replied they; for we could not chuse but laugh, when we heard of a colourless Body. Why, said the Empress, Colour is onely an accident, which is an immaterial thing, and has no being of it self, but in another body. Those, replied they, that informed your Majesty thus, surely their rational motions were very irregular; For how is it possible, that a Natural nothing can have a being in Nature? If it be no substance, it cannot have a being, and if no being, it is nothing; Wherefore the distinction between subsisting of it self, and subsisting in another body, is a meer nicety, and non-sense, for there is nothing in Nature that can subsist of, or by it self, (I mean singly) by reason all parts of Nature are composed in one body, and though they may be infinitely divided, commixed, and changed in their particular, yet in general, parts cannot be separated from parts as long as Nature lasts; nay, we might as probably affirm, that Infinite Nature would be as soon destroyed, as that one Atom could perish; and therefore your Majesty may firmly believe, that there is no Body without colour, nor no Colour without body; for colour, figure, place, magnitude, and body, are all but one thing, without any separation or abstraction from each other.

The Empress was so wonderfully taken with this Discourse of the Worm-men, that she not only pardoned the rudeness they committed in laughing at first at her question, but yielded a full assent to their opinion, which she thought the most rational that ever she had heard yet; and then proceeding in her questions, enquired further, whether they had observed any seminal principles within the Earth free from all dimensions and qualities, which produced Vegetables, Minerals, and the like? To which they answered, That concerning the seeds of Minerals, their sensitive perceptions had never observed any; but Vegetables had certain seeds out of which they were produced. Then she asked, whether those seeds of Vegetables lost their Species, that is, were annihilated in the production of their off-spring? To which they answered, That by an Annihilation, nothing could be produced, and that the seeds of Vegetables were so far from being annihilated in their productions, that they did rather numerously increase and multiply; for the division of one seed, said they, does produce numbers of seeds out of it self. But repli'd the Empress, A particular part cannot increase of it self. 'Tis true, answer'd they: but they increase not barely of themselves, but by joining and commixing with other parts, which do assist them in their productions, and by way of imitation form or figure their own parts into such or such particulars.

Then, I pray inform me, said the Empress, what disguise those seeds put on, and how they do conceal themselves in their Transmutations? They answered, That seeds did no ways disguise or conceal, but rather divulge themselves in the multiplication of their off-spring; onely they did hide and conceal themselves from their sensitive perceptions so, that their figurative and productive motions were not perceptible by Animal Creatures. Again, the Empress asked them, whether there were any Non-beings within the Earth? To which they answered, That they never heard of any such thing; and that, if her Majesty would know the truth thereof, she must ask those Creatures that are called Immaterial spirits, which had a great affinity with Non-beings, and perhaps could give her a satisfactory answer to this question. Then she desired to be informed, What opinion they had of the beginning of Forms? They told her Majesty, That they did not understand what she meant by this expression; For, said they, there is no beginning in Nature, no not of Particulars; by reason Nature is Eternal and Infinite, and her particulars are subject to infinite changes and transmutations by vertue of their own Corporeal, figurative self-motions; so that there's nothing new in Nature, not properly a beginning of any thing. The Empress seem'd well satisfied with all those answers, and enquired further, Whether there was no Art used by those Creatures that live within the Earth? Yes, answered they: for the several parts of the Earth do join and assist each other in composition or framing of such or such particulars; and many times, there are factions and divisions; which cause productions of mixt Species; as, for example, weeds, instead of sweet flowres and useful fruits; but Gardeners and Husbandmen use often to decide their quarrels, and cause them to agree; which though it shews a kindness to the differing parties, yet 'tis a great prejudice to the Worms, and other Animal-Creatures that live under ground; for it most commonly causes their dissolution and ruine, at best they are driven out of their habitations. What, said the Empress, are not Worms produced out of the Earth? Their production in general, answered they, is like the production of all other Natural Creatures, proceeding from the corporeal figurative motions of Nature; but as for their particular productions, they are according to the nature of their Species; some are produced out of flowers, some out of roots, some out of fruits, some out of ordinary Earth. Then they are very ungrateful Children, replied the Empress, that they feed on their own Parents which gave them life. Their life, answered they, is their own, and not their Parents; for no part or creature of Nature can either give or take away life; but parts do onely assist and join with parts, either in dissolution or production of other Parts and Creatures.

After this, and several other Conferences, which the Empress held with the Worm-men, she dismissed them; and having taken much satisfaction in several of their Answers, encouraged them in their Studies and Observations. Then she made a Convocation of her Chymists, the Ape-men; and commanded them to give her an account of the several Transmutations which their Art was able to produce. They begun first with a long and tedious Discourse concerning the Primitive Ingredients of Natural bodies; and how, by their Art, they had found out the principles out of which they consist. But they did not all agree in their opinions; for some said, That the Principles of all Natural Bodies were the four Elements, Fire, Air, Water, Earth, out of which they were composed: Others rejected this Elementary commixture, and said, There were many Bodies out of which none of the four Elements could be extracted by any degree of Fire whatsoever; and that, on the other side, there were divers Bodies, whose resolution by Fire reduced them into more then four different Ingredients; and these affirmed, That the only principles of Natural Bodies were Salt, Sulphur, and Mercury: Others again declared, That none of the forementioned could be called the True Principles of Natural Bodies; but that by their industry and pains which they had taken in the Art of Chymistry, they had discovered, that all Natural Bodies were produced but from one Principle, which was Water; for all Vegetables, Minerals, and Animals, said they, are nothing else, but simple Water distinguished into various figures by the vertue of their Seeds. But after a great many debates and contentions about this Subject, the Empress being so much tired that she was not able to hear them any longer, imposed a general silence upon them, and then declared her self in this following Discourse.

I am too sensible of the pains you have taken in the Art of Chymistry, to discover the Principles of Natural Bodies, and wish they had been more profitably bestowed upon some other, then such experiments; for both by my own Contemplation, and the Observations which I have made by my rational & sensitive perception upon Nature, and her works, I find, that Nature is but one Infinite Self-moving Body, which by the vertue of its self-motion, is divided into Infinite parts, which parts being restless, undergo perpetual changes and transmutations by their infinite compositions and divisions. Now, if this be so, as surely, according to regular Sense and Reason, it appears no otherwise; it is in vain to look for primary Ingredients, or constitutive principles of Natural Bodies, since there is no more but one Universal Principle of Nature, to wit, self-moving Matter, which is the onely cause of all natural effects. Next, I desire you to consider, that Fire is but a particular Creature, or effect of Nature, and occasions not onely different effects in several Bodies, but on some Bodies has no power at all; witness Gold, which never could be brought yet to change its interior figure by the art of Fire; and if this be so, Why should you be so simple as to believe that Fire can shew you the Principles of Nature? and that either the Four Elements, or Water onely, or Salt Sulphur and Mercury, all which are no more but particular effects and Creatures of Nature, should be the Primitive Ingredients or Principles of all Natural Bodies? Wherefore, I will not have you to take more pains, and waste your time in such fruitless attempts, but be wiser hereafter, and busie your selves with such Experiments as may be beneficial to the publick.

The Empress having thus declared her mind to the Ape-men, and given them better Instructions then perhaps they expected, not knowing that her Majesty had such great and able judgment in Natural Philosophy, had several conferences with them concerning Chymical Preperations, which for brevities sake, I'le forbear to reherse: Amongst the rest, she asked, how it came that the Imperial Race appear'd so young, and yet was reported to have lived so long; some of them two, some three, and some four hundred years? and whether it was by Nature, or a special Divine blessing? To which they answered, That there was a certain Rock in the parts of that World, which contained the Golden Sands, which Rock was hallow within, and did produce a Gum that was a hundred years before it came to its full strength and perfection; this Gum, said they, if it be held in a warm hand, will dissolve into an Oyl, the effects whereof are following: It being given every day for some certain time, to an old decayed man, in the bigness of a little Pea, will first make him spit for a week, or more; after this, it will cause Vomits of Flegm; and after that it will bring forth by vomits, humors of several colours; first of a pale yellow, then of a deep yellow, then of a green, and lastly of a black colour; and each of these humours have a several taste, some are fresh, some salt, some sower, some bitter, and so forth; neither do all these Vomits make them sick, but they come out on a sudden, and unawares, without any pain or trouble to the patient: And after it hath done all these mentioned effects, and clear'd both the Stomack and several other parts of the body, then it works upon the Brain, and brings forth of the Nose such kinds of humors as it did out of the Mouth, and much after the same manner; then it will purge by stool, then by urine, then by sweat, and lastly by bleeding at the Nose, and the Emeroids; all which effects it will perform within the space of six weeks, or a little more; for it does not work very strongly, but gently, and by degrees: Lastly, when it has done all this, it will make the body break out into a thick Scab, and cause both Hair, Teeth, and Nails to come off; which scab being arrived to its full maturity, opens first along the back, and comes off all in a piece like armour, and all this is done within the space of four months. After this the Patient is wrapt into a Cere-cloth, prepared of certain Gums and Juices, wherein he continues until the time of nine Months be expired from the first beginning of the cure, which is the time of a Childs formation in the Womb. In the mean while, his diet is nothing else but Eagles-eggs, and Hinds-milk; and after the Cere-cloth is taken away, he will appear of the age of Twenty, both in shape, and strength. The weaker sort of this Gum is soveraign in healing of wounds, and curing of slight distempers. But this is also to be observed, that none of the Imperial race does use any other drink but Lime-water, or water in which Lime-stone is immerged; their meat is nothing else but Fowl of several sorts, their recreations are many, but chiefly Hunting.

This Relation amazed the Empress very much; for though in the World she came from, she had heard great reports of the Philosophers-stone, yet had she not heard of any that had ever found it out, which made her believe that it was but a Chymera; she called also to mind, that there had been in the same World a Man who had a little Stone which cured all kinds of Diseases outward and inward, according it was applied; and that a famous Chymist had found out a certain Liquor called Alkahest, which by the vertue of its own fire, consumed all Diseases; but she had never heard of a Medicine that could renew old Age, and render it beautiful, vigorous and strong: Nor would she have so easily believed it, had it been a medicine prepared by Art; for she knew that Art, being Natures Changeling, was not able to produce such a powerful effect; but being that the Gum did grow naturally, she did not so much scruple at it; for she knew that Nature's Works are so various and wonderful, that no particular Creature is able to trace her ways.

The Conferences of the Chymists being finished, the Empress made an Assembly of her Galenical Physicians, her Herbalists and Anatomists; and first she enquired of her Herbalists the particular effects of several Herbs and Drugs, and whence they proceeded? To which they answered, that they could, for the most part, tell her Majesty the vertues and operations of them, but the particular causes of their effects were unknown; onely thus much they could say, that their operations and vertues were generally caused by their proper inherent, corporeal, figurative motions, which being infinitely various in Infinite Nature, did produce infinite several effects. And it is observed, said they, that Herbs and Drugs are as wise in their operations, as Men in their words and actions; nay, wiser; and their effects are more certain then Men in their opinions; for though they cannot discourse like Men, yet have they Sense and Reason, as well as Men; for the discursive faculty is but a particular effect of Sense and Reason in some particular Creatures, to wit, Men, and not a principle of Nature, and argues often more folly then wisdom. The Empress asked, Whether they could not by a composition and commixture of other Drugs make them work other effects then they did, used by themselves? They answered, That they could make them produce artificial effects, but not alter their inherent, proper and particular natures.

Then the Empress commanded her Anatomists to dissect such kinds of Creatures as are called Monsters. But they answered her Majesty, That it would be but an unprofitable and useless work, and hinder their better imployments; for when we dissect dead Animals, said they, it is for no other end, but to observe what defects and distempers they had, that we may cure the like in living ones, so that all our care and industry concerns onely the preservation of Mankind; but we hope your Majesty will not preserve Monsters, which are most commonly destroyed, except it be for novelty: Neither will the dissection of Monsters prevent the errors of Nature's irregular actions; for by dissecting some, we cannot prevent the production of others; so that our pains and labour will be to no purpose, unless to satisfie the vain curiosities of inquisitive men. The Empress replied, That such dissections would be very beneficial to Experimental Philosophers. If Experimental Philosophers, answer'd they, do spend their time in such useless Inspections, they waste it in vain, and have nothing but their labour for their pains.

Lastly, her Majesty had some Conferences with the Galenick Physicians about several Diseases, and amongst the rest, desired to know the cause and nature of Apoplexies, and the spotted Plague. They answered, That a deadly Apoplexy was a dead palsie of the Brain, and the spotted Plague was a Gangrene of the Vital parts: and as the Gangrene of outward parts did strike inwardly; so the Gangrene of inward parts, did break forth outwardly: which is the cause, said they, that as soon as the spots appear, death follows; for then it is an infallible sign, that the body is throughout infected with a Gangrene, which is a spreading evil; but some Gangrenes do spread more suddenly than others, and of all sorts of Gangrenes, the Plaguy-Gangrene is the most infectious; for other Gangrenes infect but the next adjoining parts of one particular body, and having killed that same Creature, go no further, but cease; when as, the Gangrene of the Plague, infects not onely the adjoining parts of one particular Creature, but also those that are distant; that is, one particular body infects another, and so breeds a Universal Contagion. But the Empress being very desirous to know in what manner the Plague was propagated, and became so contagious, asked, Whether it went actually out of one body into another? To which they answered, That it was a great dispute amongst the Learned of their Profession, Whether it came by a division and composition of parts; that is, by expiration and inspiration; or whether it was caused by imitation: some Experimental Philosophers, said they, will make us believe, that by the help of their Microscopes, they have observed the Plague to be a body of little Flies like Atoms, which go out of one body into another, through the sensitive passages; but the most experienced and wisest of our society, have rejected this opinion as a ridiculous fancy, and do, for the most part, believe, that it is caused by an imitation of Parts; so that the motions of some parts which are sound, do imitate the motions of those that are infected and that by this means, the Plague becomes contagions, and spreading.

The Empress having hitherto spent her time in the Examination of the Bird- Fish- Worm- and Ape-men, &c. and received several Intelligences from their several imployments; at last had a mind to divert her self after her serious Discourses, and therefore she sent for the Spider-men, which were her Mathematicians, the Lice-men which were here Geometricians, and the Magpie- Parrot- and Jackdaw-men, which were her Orators and Logicians. The Spider-men came first, and presented her Majesty with a table full of Mathematical points, lines, and figures of all sorts, of squares, circles, triangles, and the like; which the Empress, notwithstanding that she had a very ready wit, and quick apprehension, could not understand; but the more she endeavoured to learn, the more was she confounded: Whether they did ever square the Circle, I cannot exactly tell, nor whether they could make imaginary points and lines; but this I dare say, That their points and lines were so slender, small and thin, that they seem'd next to Imaginary. The Mathematicians were in great esteem with the Empress, as being not onely the chief Tutors and Instructors in many Arts, but some of them excellent Magicians and Informers of spirits, which was the reason their Characters were so abstruse and intricate, that the Emperess knew not what to make of them. There is so much to learn in your Art, said she, that I can neither spare time from other affairs to busie my self in your profession; nor, if I could, do I think I should ever be able to understand your Imaginary points, lines and figures, because they are Non-beings.

Then came the Lice-men, and endeavoured to measure all things to a hairs-breadth, and weigh them to an Atom; but their weights would seldom agree, especially in the weighing of Air, which they found a task impossible to be done; at which the Empress began to be displeased, and told them, that there was neither Truth nor Justice in their Profession; and so dissolved their society.

After this, the Empress was resolved to hear the Magpie- Parrot- and Jackdaw-men, which were her professed Orators and Logicians; whereupon one of the Parrot-men rose with great formality, and endeavoured to make an Eloquent Speech before her Majesty; but before he had half ended, his arguments and divisions being so many, that they caused a great confusion in his brain, he could not go forward, but was forced to retire backward, with great disgrace both to himself, and the whole society; and although one of his brethren endeavoured to second him by another speech, yet was he as far to seek, as the former. At which the Empress appear'd not a little troubled, and told them, That they followed too much the Rules of Art, and confounded themselves with too nice formalities and distinctions; but since I know, said she, that you are a people who have naturally voluble tongues, and good memories; I desire you to consider more the subject you speak of, then your artificial periods, connexions and parts of speech, and leave the rest to your natural Eloquence; which they did, and so became very eminent Orators.

Lastly, her Imperial Majesty being desirous to know what progress her Logicians had made in the Art of disputing, Commanded them to argue upon several Themes or Subjects; which they did; and having made a very nice discourse of Logistical terms and propositions, entred into a dispute by way of Syllogistical Arguments, through all the Figures and Modes: One began with an Argument of the first Mode of the first Figure, thus: Every Politician is wise: Every Knave is a Politician, Therefore every Knave is wise.

Another contradicted him with a Syllogism of the second Mode of the same Figure, thus: No Politician is wise: Every Knave is a Politician, Therefore no Knave is wise.

The third made an Argument in the third Mode of the same Figure, after this manner: Every Politician is wise: some Knaves are Politicians, Therefore some Knaves are wise.

The Fourth concluded with a Syllogism in the fourth Mode of the same Figure, thus; No Politician is wise: some Knaves are Politicians, Therefore some Knaves are not wise.

After this they took another subject, and one propounded this Syllogism: Every Philosopher is wise: Every Beast is wise, Therefore every Beast is a Philosopher.

But another said that this Argument was false, therefore he contradicted him with a Syllogism of the second Figure of the fourth Mode, thus: Every Philosopher is wise: some Beasts are not wise, Therefore some Beasts are not Philosophers.

Thus they argued, and intended to go on, but the Empress interrupted them: I have enough, said she, of your chopt Logick, and will hear no more of your Syllogisms; for it disorders my Reason, and puts my Brain on the rack; your formal argumentations are able to spoil all natural wit; and I'le have you to consider, that Art does not make Reason, but Reason makes Art; and therefore as much as Reason is above Art, so much is a natural rational discourse to be preferred before an artificial: for Art is, for the most part irregular, and disorders Men's understandings more then it rectifies them, and leads them into a Labyrinth where they'l never get out, and makes them dull and unfit for useful employments; especially your

Art of Logick, which consists onely in contradicting each other, in making sophismes, and obscuring Truth, instead of clearing it.

But they replied to her Majesty, That the knowledg of Nature, that is, Natural Philosophy, would be imperfect without the Art of Logick; and that there was an improbable Truth which could no otherwise be found out then by the Art of disputing. Truly, said the Empress, I do believe that it is with Natural Philosophy, as it is with all other effects of Nature; for no particular knowledg can be perfect, by reason knowledg is dividable, as well as composable; nay, to speak properly, Nature her self cannot boast of any perfection, but God himself; because there are so many irregular motions in Nature, and 'tis but a folly to think that Art should be able to regulate them, since Art it self is, for the most part, irregular. But as for Improbable Truth I know not what your meaning is; for Truth is more then Improbability: nay, there is so much difference between Truth and Improbability, that I cannot conceive it possible how they can be joined together. In short, said she, I do no ways approve of your Profession; and though I will not dissolve your society, yet I shall never take delight in hearing you any more; wherefore confine your disputations to your Schools, lest besides the Commonwealth of Learning, they disturb also Divinity and Policy, Religion and Laws, and by that means draw an utter ruine and destruction both upon Church and State.

After the Empress had thus finish'd the Discourses and Conferences with the mentioned societies of her Vertuoso's, she considered by her self the manner of their Religion, and finding it very defective, was troubled, that so wise and knowing a people should have no more knowledg of the Divine Truth; Wherefore she consulted with her own thoughts, whether it was possible to convert them all to her own Religion, and to that end she resolved to build Churches, and make also up a Congregation of Women, whereof she intended to be the head her self, and to instruct them in the several points of her Religion. This she had no sooner begun, but the Women, which generally had quick wits, subtile conceptions, clear understandings, and solid judgments, became, in a short time, very devout and zealous Sisters; for the Empress had an excellent gift of Preaching, and instructing them in the Articles of Faith; and by that means, she converted them not onely soon, but gained an extraordinary love of all her Subjects throughout that World. But at last, pondering with her self the inconstant nature of Mankind, and fearing that in time they would grow weary, and desert the divine Truth, following their own fancies, and living according to their own desires; she began to be troubled that her labours and pains should prove of so little effect, and therefore studied all manner of ways to prevent it. Amongst the rest, she call'd to mind a Relation which the Bird-men made her once, of a Mountain that did burn in flames of fire; and thereupon did immediately send for the wisest and subtilest of her Worm-men, commanding them to discover the cause of the Eruption of that same fire; which they did; and having dived to the very bottom of the Mountain, informed her Majesty, That there was a certain sort of Stone, whose nature was such, that being wetted, it would grow excessively hot, and break forth into a flaming-fire, until it became dry, and then it ceased from burning. The Empress was glad to hear this news, and forthwith desired the Worm men to bring her some of that Stone, but be sure to keep it secret: she sent also for the Bird-men, and asked them whether they could not get her a piece of the Sun-stone? They answered, That it was impossible, unless they did spoil or lessen the light of the World: but, said they, if it please your Majesty, we can demolish one of the numerous Stars of the Sky, which the World will never miss.

The Empress was very well satisfied with this proposal, and having thus imployed these two sorts of men, in the mean while builded two Chappels one above another; the one she lined throughout with Diamonds, both Roof, Walls and Pillars; but the other she resolved to line with the Star-stone; the Fire-stone she placed upon the Diamond-lining, by reason Fire has no power on Diamonds; and when she would have that Chappel where the Fire-stone was, appear all in flame, she had by the means of Artificial pipes, water conveighed into it, which by turning the Cock, did, as out of a Fountain, spring over all the room, and as long as the Fire-stone was wet, the Chappel seemed to be all in a flaming-fire.

The other Chappel, which was lined with the Star-stone, did onely cast a splendorous and comfortable light; both the Chappels stood upon Pillars, just in the middle of a round Cloyster, which was dark as night; neither was there any other light within them, but what came from the Fire- and Star-stone; and being every where open, allowed to all that were within the compass of the Cloyster, a free prospect into them; besides, they were so artificially contrived, that they did both move in a Circle about their own Centres, without intermission, contrary ways. In the Chappel which was lined with the Fire-stone, the Empress preached Sermons of Terror to the wicked, and told them of the punishments for their sins, to wit, That after this life they should be tormented in an everlasting Fire. But in the other Chappel lined with the Star-stone, she preached Sermons of Comfort to those that repented of their sins, and were troubled at their own wickedness: Neither did the heat of the flame in the least hinder her; for the Fire-stone did not cast so great a heat but the Empress was able to endure it, by reason the water which was poured on the Stone, by its own self-motion turned into a flaming-fire, occasioned by the natural motions of the Stone, which made the flame weaker then if it had been fed by some other kind of fuel; the other Chappel where the Star-Stone was, although it did cast a great light, yet was it without all heat, and the Empress appear'd like an Angel in it; and as that Chappel was an embleme of Hell, so this was an embleme of Heaven. And thus the Empress, by Art, and her own Ingenuity, did not onely convert the Blazing-World to her own Religion, but kept them in a constant belief, without inforcement or blood-shed; for she knew well, that belief was a thing not to be forced or pressed upon the people, but to be instilled into their minds by gentle perswasions; and after this manner she encouraged them also in all other duties and employments: for Fear, though it makes people obey, yet does it not last so long, nor is it so sure a means to keep them to their duties, as Love.

Last of all, when she saw that both Church and State now in a well-ordered and setled condition, her thoughts reflected upon the World she came from; and though she had a great desire to know the condition of the same, yet could she advise no manner of way how to gain any knowledg thereof; at last, after many serious considerations, she conceived that it was impossible to be done by any other means, then by the help of Immaterial Spirits; wherefore she made a Convocation of the most learned, witty and ingenious of all the forementioned sorts of Men, and desired to know of them, whether there were any Immaterial Spirits in their World. First, she enquired of the Worm-men, whether they had perceived some within the Earth? They answered her Majesty, That they never knew of any such Creatures; for whatsoever did dwell within the Earth, said they, was imbodied and material. Then she asked the Fly-men, whether they had observed any in the Air? for you having numerous Eyes, said she, will be more able to perceive them, than any other Creatures. To which they answered her Majesty, That although Spirits, being immaterial, could not be perceived by the Worm-men in the Earth, yet they perceived that such Creatures did lodg in the Vehicles of the Air. Then the Empress asked, Whether they could speak to them, and whether they did understand each other? The Fly-men answered, That those Spirits were always cloth'd in some sort or other of Material Garments; which Garments were their Bodies, made, for the most part, of Air; and when occasion served, they could put on any other sort of substances; but yet they could not put these substances into any form or shape, as they pleased. The Empress asked the Fly-men, whether it was possible that she could be acquainted, and have some conferences with them?

They answered, They did verily believe she might. Hereupon the Empress commanded the Fly-men to ask some of the Spirits, Whether they would be pleased to give her a Visit? This they did; and after the Spirits had presented themselves to the Empress, (in what shapes and forms, I cannot exactly tell) after some few Complements that passed between them, the Empress told the Spirits that she questioned not, but they did know how she was a stranger in that World, and by what miraculous means she was arrived there; and since she had a great desire to know the condition of the World she came from, her request to the Spirits was, To give her some Information thereof, especially of those parts of the World where she was born, bred, and educated; as also of her particular friends and acquaintance: all which, the Spirits did according to her desire. At last, after a great many conferences and particular intelligences, which the Spirits gave the Empress, to her great satisfaction and content; she enquired after the most famous Students, Writers, and Experimental Philosophers in that World, which they gave her full relation of: amongst the rest she enquired, Whether there were none that had found out yet the Jews Cabbala? Several have endeavoured it, answered the Spirits, but those that came nearest (although themselves denied it) were one Dr. Dee, and one Edward Kelly, the one representing Moses, and the other Aaron; for Kelly was to Dr. Dee, as Aaron to Moses; but yet they proved at last but meer Cheats; and were described by one of their own Country-men, a famous Poet, named Ben. Johnson, in a Play call'd, The Alchymist, where he expressed Kelly by Capt. Face, and Dee by Dr. Subtle, and their two Wives by Doll Common, and the Widow; by the Spaniard the Play, he meant the Spanish Ambassador, and by Sir Epicure Mammon, a Polish Lord. The Empress remembred that she had seen the Play, and asked the Spirits, whom he meant by the name of Ananias? some Zealous Brethren, answered they, in Holland, Germany, and several other places. Then she asked them, Who was meant by the Druggist? Truly, answered the Spirits, We have forgot, it being so long since it was made and acted. What, replied the Empress, Can Spirits forget? Yes, said the Spirits; for what is past, is onely kept in memory, if it be not recorded. I did believe, said the Empress, That Spirits had no need of Memory, or Remembrance, and could not be subject to Forgetfulness. How can we, answered they, give an account of things present, if we had no Memory, but especially of things past, unrecorded, if we had no Remembrance? said the Empress, By present Knowledg and Understanding. The Spirits answered, That present Knowledg and Understanding was of actions or things present, not of past. But, said the Empress, you know what is to come, without Memory or Remembrance; and therefore you may know what is past without memory and remembrance. They answered, That their foreknowledg was onely a prudent and subtile Observation made by comparing of things or actions past, with those that are present; and that Remembrance was nothing else but a Repetition of things or actions past.

Then the Empress asked the Spirits, Whether there was a threefold Cabbala? They answered, Dee and Kelly made but a two-fold Cabbala, to wit, of the Old and New Testament, but others might not onely make two or three, but threescore Cabbala's, if they pleased. The Empress asked, Whether it was a Traditional, or meerly a Scriptural, or whether it was a Literal, Philosophical, or Moral Cabbala some, answered they, did believe it meerly Traditional, others Scriptural, some Literal, and some Metaphorical: but the truth is, said they, 'twas partly one, and partly the other; as partly a Traditional, partly a Scriptural, partly Literal, partly Metaphorical. The Empress asked further, Whether the Cabbala was a work onely of Natural Reason, or of Divine Inspiration? Many, said the Spirits, that write Cabbala's pretend to Divine Inspirations; but whether it be so, or not, it does not belong to us to judg; onely this we must needs confess, that it is a work which requires a good wit, and a strong Faith, but not Natural Reason; for though Natural Reason is most perswasive, yet Faith is the chief that is required in Cabbalists. But, said the Empress, Is there not Divine Reason, as well as there is Natural? No, answered they: for there is but a Divine Faith, and as for Reason it is onely Natural; but you Mortals are so puzled about this Divine Faith, and Natural Reason, that you do not know well how to distinguish them, but confound them both, which is the cause you have so many divine Philosophers who make a Gallimafry both of Reason and Faith. Then she asked, Whether pure Natural Philosophers were Cabbalists? They answered, No; but onely your Mystical or Divine Philosophers, such as study beyond Sense and Reason. she enquired further, Whether there was any Cabbala in God, or whether God was full of Idea's? They answered, There could be nothing in God, nor could God be full of any thing, either forms or figures, but of himself; for God is the Perfection of all things, and an Unexpressible Being, beyond the conception of any Creature, either Natural or Supernatural. Then I pray inform me, said the Empress, Whether the Jews Cabbala or any other, consist in Numbers? The Spirits answered, No: for Numbers are odd, and different, and would make a disagreement in the Cabbala. But, said she again, Is it a sin then not to know or understand the Cabbala? God is so merciful, answered they, and so just, that he will never damn the ignorant, and save onely those that pretend to know him and his secret Counsels by their Cabbala's; but he loves those that adore and worship him with fear and reverence, and with a pure heart. she asked further, which of these two Cabbala's was most approved, the Natural, or Theological? The Theological, answered they, is mystical, and belongs onely to Faith; but the Natural belongs to Reason. Then she asked them, Whether Divine Faith was made out of Reason? No answered they, for Faith proceeds onely from a Divine saving Grace, which is a peculiar Gift of God. How comes it then, replied she, that Men, even those that are of several opinions, have Faith more or less? A Natural Belief, answered they, is not a Divine Faith. But, proceeded the Empress, How are you sure that God cannot be known? The several Opinions you Mortals have of God, answered they, are sufficient witnesses thereof. Well then, replied the Empress, leaving this inquisitive knowledg of God, I pray inform me, whether you Spirits give motion to Natural Bodies? No, answered they; but, on the contrary, Natural material bodies give Spirits motion; for we Spirits, being incorporeal, have no motion but from our Corporeal Vehicles, so that we move by the help of our Bodies, and not the Bodies by our help; for pure Spirits are immovable. If this be so, replied the Empress, How comes it then that you can move so suddenly at a vast distance? They answered, That some sorts of matter were more pure, rare, and consequently more light and agil then others; and this was the reason for their quick and sudden motions. Then the Empress asked them, Whether they could speak without a body, or bodily organs? No, said they; nor could we have any bodily sense, but onely knowledg. she asked, Whether they could have Knowledg without Body? Not a Natural, answered they, but a Supernatural Knowledg, which is a far better Knowledg then a Natural. Then she asked them, Whether they had a General or Universal Knowledg? They answered, Single or particular created Spirits, have not; for not any Creature, but God Himself, can have an absolute and perfect knowledg of all things. The Empress asked them further, Whether Spirits had inward and outward parts? No, answered they; for parts onely belong to bodies, not to Spirits. Again, she asked them, Whether their Vehicles were living Bodies? They are Self-moving Bodies, answered they, and therefore they must needs be living; for nothing can move it self, without it hath life. Then, said she, it must necessarily follow, that this living, Self-moving Body gives motion to the Spirit, and not the Spirit motion to the Body, as its Vehicle. You say very true, answered they, and we told you this before. Then the Empress asked them, Of what forms of Matter those Vehicles were? They said they were of several different forms; some gross and dense, and others more pure, rare, and subtil. If you be not Material, said the Empress, how can you be Generators of all Creatures? We are no more, answered they, the Generators of material Creatures, then they are the Generators of us Spirits. Then she asked, Whether they did leave their Vehicles? No, answered they; for we being incorporeal, cannot leave or quit them: but our Vehicles do change into several forms and figures, according as occasion requires. Then the Empress desired the Spirits to tell her, Whether Man was a little World? They answered, That if a Fly or Worm was a little World, then Man was so too. she asked again, Whether our Fore-fathers had been as wise, as Men were at present, and had understood sense and reason, as well as they did now? They answered, That in former Ages they had been as wise as they are in this present, nay, wiser; for, said they, many in this age do think their Fore-fathers have been Fools, by which they prove themselves to be such. The Empress asked further, Whether there was any Plastick power in Nature? Truly, said the Spirits, Plastick power is a hard word, & signifies no more then the power of the corporeal, figurative motions of Nature. After this, the

Empress desired the Spirits to inform her where the Paradise was, Whether it was in the midst of the World as a Centre of pleasure? or, Whether it was the whole World; or a peculiar World by it self, as a World of Life, and not of Matter; or whether it was mixt, as a world of living animal Creatures? They answered, That Paradise was not in the world she came from, but in that world she lived in at present; and that it was the very same place where she kept her Court, and where her Palace stood, in the midst of the Imperial City. The Empress asked further, Whether in the beginning and Creation of the World, all Beasts could speak? They answered, That no Beasts could speak, but onely those sorts of Creatures which were Fish-men, Bear-men, Worm-men, and the like, which could speak in the first Age, as well as they do now. she asked again, Whether they were none of those Spirits that frighted Adam out of the Paradise, at least caused him not to return thither again? They an? swered they were not. Then she desired to be informed, whither Adam fled when he was driven out of the Paradise? Out of this World, said they, you are now Empress of, into the World you came from. If this be so, replied the Empress, then surely those Cabbalists are much out of their story, who believe the Paradise to be a world of Life onely, without Matter, for this world, though it be most pleasant and fruitful, yet it is not a world of meer Immaterial life, but a world of living, Material Creatures. Without question, they are, answered the Spirits; for not all Cabbala's are true. Then the Empress asked, That since it is mentioned in the story of the Creation of the World, that Eve was tempted by the Serpent, Whether the Devil was within the Serpent, or, Whether the Serpent tempted her without the Devil? They answered, That the Devil was within the Serpent. But how came it then, replied she, that the Serpent was cursed? They answered, because the Devil was in him; for are not those men in danger of damnation which have the Devil within them, who perswades them to believe and act wickedly? The Empress asked further, Whether Light and the Heavens were all one? They answered, That that Region which contains the Lucid natural Orbs, was by Mortals named Heaven; but the Beatifical Heaven, which is the Habitation of the Blessed Angels and Souls, was so far beyond it, that it could not be compared to any Natural Creature. Then the Empress asked them, Whether all Matter was fluid at first? They answered, That Matter was always as it is, and that some parts of Matter were rare, some dense, some fluid, some solid, &c. Neither was

God bound to make all Matter fluid at first. she asked further, Whether Matter was immovable in it self? We have answered you before, said they, That there is no motion but in Matter; and were it not for the motion of Matter, we Spirits, could not move, nor give you any answer to your several questions. After this, the Empress asked the Spirits, Whether the Universe was made within the space of six days, or, Whether by those six days, were meant so many Decrees or Commands of God? They answered her, That the World was made by the All-powerful Decree and Command of God; but whether there were six Decrees or Commands, or fewer, or more, no Creature was able to tell.

Then she inquired, Whether there was no mystery in Numbers? No other mystery, answered the Spirits, but reckoning or counting; for Numbers are onely marks of remembrance. But what do you think of the Number of Four, said she, which Cabbalists make such ado withal, and of the Number of Ten, when they say that Ten is all, and that all Numbers are virtually comprehended in Four? We think, answered they, that Cabbalists have nothing else to do but to trouble their heads with such useless Fancies; for naturally there is no such thing as prime or all in Numbers; nor is there any other mystery in Numbers, but what Man's fancy makes; but what Men call Prime, or All, we do not know, because they do not agree in the number of their opinion. Then the Empress asked, Whether the number of six was a symbole of Matrimony, as being made up of Male and Femal, for two into three is six. If any number can be a symbole of Matrimony, answered the Spirits, it is not Six, but Two; if two may be allowed to be a Number: for the act of Matrimony is made up of two joined in one. she asked again, What they said to the number of Seven? whether it was not an Embleme of God, because Cabbalists say, That it is neither begotten, nor begets any other Number? There can be no Embleme of God, answered the Spirits; for if we do not know what God is, how can we make an Embleme of him? Nor is there any Number in God, for God is the perfection Himself; but Numbers are imperfect; and as for the begetting of numbers, it is done by Multiplication and Addition; but Substraction is as a kind of death to Numbers. If there be no mystery in Numbers, replied the Empress then it is in vain to refer to the Creation of the World to certain Numbers, as Cabbalists do. The onely mystery of Numbers, answered they, concerning the Creation of the World, is, that as Numbers do multiply, so does the World. The Empress asked, how far

Numbers did multiply? The Spirits answered, to Infinite. Why, said she, Infinite cannot be reckoned, nor numbred. No more, answered they, can the parts of the Universe; for God's Creation, being an Infinite action, as proceeding from an Infinite Power, could not rest upon a finite Number of Creatures, were it never so great. But leaving the mystery of Numbers, proceeded the Empress, Let me now desire you to inform me, Whether the Suns and Planets were generated by the Heavens, or Æthereal Matter? The Spirits answered, That the Stars and Planets were of the same matter which the Heavens, the Æther, and all other Natural Creatures did consist of; but whether they were generated by the Heavens or Æther, they could not tell: if they be, said they, they are not like their Parents; for the Sun, Stars, and Planets, are more splendorous then the Æther, as also more solid and constant in their motions: But put the case, the Stars and Planets were generated by the Heavens, and the Æthereal Matter; the question then would be, Out of what these are generated or produced? If these be created out of nothing, and not generated out of something, then it is probable the Sun, Stars and Planets are so too; nay, it is more probable of the Stars, and Planets, then of the Heavens, or the fluid Æther, by reason the Stars and Planets seem to be further off from Mortality, then the particular parts of the Æther; for no doubt but the parts of the Æthereal Matter, alter into several forms, which we do not perceive of the Stars and Planets. The Empress asked further, Whether they could give her information of the three principles of Man, according to the doctrine of the Platonists; as first of the Intellect, Spirit, or Divine Light. 2. Of the Soul of Man her self: and 3. Of the Image of the Soul, that is, her vital operation on the body? The Spirits answered, That they did not understand these three distinctions, but that they seem'd to corporeal sense and reason, as if they were three several bodies, or three several corporeal actions; however, said they, they are intricate conceptions of irregular Fancies. If you do not understand them, replied the Empress, how shall human Creatures do then? Many, both of your modern and ancient Philosophers, answered the Spirits, endeavour to go beyond Sense and Reason, which makes them commit absurdities; for no corporeal Creature can go beyond Sense and Reason; no not we Spirits, as long as we are in our corporeal Vehicles. Then the Empress asked them, Whether there were any Atheists in the World? The Spirits answered, That there were no more Atheists then what Cabbalists make. she asked them further,

Whether Spirits were of a globous or round Figure? They answered, That Figure belonged to body, but they being immaterial, had no Figure. she asked again, Whether Spirits were not like Water or Fire? They answered, that Water and Fire was material, were it the purest and most refined that ever could be; nay, were it above the Heavens: But we are no more like Water or Fire, said they, then we are like Earth; but our Vehicles are of several forms, figures and degrees of substances. Then she desired to know, Whether their Vehicles were made of Air? Yes, answered the Spirits, some of our Vehicles are of thin Air. Then I suppose, replied the Empress, That those airy Vehicles, are your corporeal Summer-suits. she asked further, Whether the Spirits had not ascending and descending-motions, as well as other Creatures? They answered, That properly there was no ascension or descension in Infinite Nature, but onely in relation to particular parts; and as for us Spirits, said they, We can neither ascend nor descend without corporeal Vehicles; nor can our Vehicles ascend or descend, but according to their several shapes and figures, for there can be no motion without body. The Empress asked them further, Whether there was not a World of Spirits, as well as there is of Material Creatures? No, answered they; for the word World implies a quantity or multitude of corporeal Creatures, but we being Immaterial, can make no World of Spirits. Then she desired to be informed when Spirits were made? We do not know, answered they, how and when we were made, nor are we much inquisitive after it; nay, if we did, it would be no benefit, neither for us, nor for you Mortals to know it. The Empress replied, That Cabbalists and Divine Philosophers said, Mens rational Souls were Immaterial, and stood as much in need of corporeal Vehicles, as Spirits did. If this be so, answered the Spirits, then you are Hermaphrodites of Nature; but your Cabbalists are mistaken, for they take the purest and subtilest parts of Matter, for Immaterial Spirits. Then the Empress asked, When the Souls of Mortals went out of their Bodies, whether they went to Heaven or Hell; or whether, they remained in airy Vehicles? God's Justice and Mercy, answered they, is perfect, and not imperfect; but if you Mortals will have Vehicles for your Souls, and a place that is between Heaven and Hell, it must be Purgatory, which is a place of Purification, for which action Fire is more proper then Air; and so the Vehicles of those Souls that are in Purgatory, cannot be airy, but fiery; and after this rate there can be but four places for human Souls to be in, viz. Heaven, Hell, Purgatory, and this

World; but as for Vehicles, they are but fancies, not real truths. Then the Empress asked them, Where Heaven and Hell was? Your Saviour Christ, answered the Spirits, has informed you, that there is Heaven and Hell, but he did not tell you what, nor where they are; wherefore it is too great a presumption for you Mortals to inquire after it: If you do but strive to get into Heaven, it is enough, though you do not know where or what it is; for it is beyond your knowledg and understanding. I am satisfied, replied the Empress; and asked further, Whether there were any Figures or Characters in the Soul? They answered, Where there was no Body, there could be no Figure. Then she asked them, Whether Spirits could be naked? and whether they were of a dark, or a light colour? As for our Nakedness, it is a very odd question, answered the Spirits; and we do not know what you mean by a Naked Spirit; for you judg of us as of corporeal Creatures; and as for Colour, said they, it is according to our Vehicles; for Colour belongs to Body, and as there is no Body that is colourless, so there is no Colour that is bodiless. Then the Empress desired to be informed, Whether all Souls were made at the first Creation of the World? We know no more, answered the Spirits, of the origin of humane Souls, then we know of our Selves. she asked further, Whether humane bodies were not burthensome to humane Souls? They answered, That Bodies, made Souls active, as giving them motion; and if action was troublesome to Souls, then Bodies were so too. she asked again, Whether Souls did chuse Bodies? They answered, That Platonicks believed, the Souls of Lovers lived in the Bodies of their Beloved, but surely, said they, if there be a multitude of Souls in a World of Matter, they cannot miss Bodies; for as soon as a Soul is parted from one Body, it enters into another; and Souls having no motion of themselves, must of necessity be clothed or imbodied with the next parts of Matter. If this be so, replied the Empress, then I pray inform me, Whether all matter be soulified? The Spirits answered, They could not exactly tell that; but if it was true, that Matter had no other motion but what came from a spiritual power, and that all matter was moving, then no soul could quit a Body, but she must, of necessity enter into another soulified Body, and then there would be two immaterial substances in one Body. The Empress asked, Whether it was not possible that there could be two Souls in one Body? As for Immaterial Souls, answered the Spirits, it is impossible; for there cannot be two Immaterials in one Inanimate Body, by reason they want parts, and place, being bodiless; but there may be numerous material Souls in one composed Body, by reason every material part has a material natural Soul; for Nature is but one Infinite self-moving, living and self-knowing body, consisting of the three degrees of inanimate, sensitive and rational Matter, so intermixt together, that no part of Nature, were it an Atom, can be without any of these three Degrees; the sensitive is the Life, the rational the Soul, and the inanimate part, the Body of Infinite Nature. The Empress was very well satisfied with this answer, and asked further, Whether souls did not give life to bodies? No, answered they; but Spirits and Divine Souls have a life of their own, which is not to be divided, being purer then a natural life; for Spirits are incorporeal, and consequently indivisible. But when the Soul is in its Vehicle, said the Empress, then methinks she is like the Sun, and the Vehicle like the Moon. No, answered they; but the Vehicle is like the Sun, and the Soul like the Moon; for the Soul hath motion from the Body, as the Moon has light from the Sun. Then the Empress asked the Spirits, Whether it was an evil Spirit that tempted Eve, and brought all the mischiefs upon Mankind: or, Whether it was the Serpent? They answered, That Spirits could not commit actual evils. The Empress said, they might do it by perswasions. They answered, That Perswasions were actions; But the Empress not being contented with this answer, asked, Whether there was not a supernatural Evil? The Spirits answered, That there was a Supernatural Good, which was God; but they knew of no Supernatural Evil, that was equal to God. Then she desired to know, Whether Evil Spirits were reckoned amongst the Beasts of the Field? They answer'd, That many Beasts of the field were harmless Creatures, and very serviceable for Man's use; and though some were accounted fierce and cruel, yet did they exercise their cruelty upon other Creatures, for the most part, to no other end, but to get themselves food, and to satisfie their natural appetite; but certainly, said they, you Men are more cruel to one another, then evil Spirits are to you; and as for their habitations in desolate places, we having no communion with them, can give you no certain account thereof. But what do you think, said the Empress, of good Spirits? may not they be compared to the Fowls of the Air? They answered, There were many cruel and ravenous Fowls as well in the Air, as there were fierce and cruel Beasts on Earth; so that the good are always mixt with the bad. she asked further, Whether the fiery Vehicles were a Heaven, or a Hell, or at least a Purgatory to the Souls? They answered, That if the Souls were immaterial, they could not burn, and then fire would do them no harm; and though Hell was believed to be an undecaying and unquenchable fire, yet Heaven was no fire. The Empress replied, That Heaven was a Light. Yes, said they, but not a fiery Light. Then she asked, Whether the different shapes and sorts of Vehicles, made the Souls and other Immaterial Spirits, miserable, or blessed? The Vehicles, answered they, make them neither better, nor worse; for though some Vehicles sometimes may have power over others, yet these by turns may get some power again over them, according to the several advantages and disadvantages of particular Natural parts. The Empress asked further, Whether Animal life came out of the spiritual World, and did return thither again? The Spirits answered, They could not exactly tell; but if it were so, then certainly Animal lives must leave their bodies behind them, otherwise the bodies would make the spiritual World a mixt World, that is, partly material, and partly immaterial; but the Truth is, said they, Spirits being immaterial, cannot properly make a World; for a World belongs to material, not to immaterial Creatures. If this be so, replied the Empress, then certainly there can be no world of Lives and Forms without Matter? No, answered the Spirits; nor a world of Matter without Lives and Forms; for Natural Lives and Forms cannot be immaterial, no more then Matter can be immovable. And therefore natural lives, forms and matter, are inseparable. Then the Empress asked, Whether the first Man did feed on the best sorts of the Fruits of the Earth, and the Beasts on the worst? The Spirits answered, That unless the Beasts of the field were barred out of manured fields and gardens, they would pick and chuse the best Fruits as well as Men; and you may plainly observe it, said they, in Squirrels and Monkies, how they are the best Chusers of Nuts and Apples; and how Birds do pick and feed in the most delicious fruits, and Worms on the best roots, and most savoury herbs; by which you may see, that those Creatures live and feed better then men do, except you will say, that artificial Cookery is better and more wholsome then the natural. Again, the Empress asked, Whether the first Man gave Names to all the several sorts of Fishes in the Sea, and fresh Waters? No, answered the Spirits, for he was an Earthly, and not a Watery Creature; and therefore could not know the several sorts of Fishes. Why, replied the Empress, he was no more an Airy Creature then he was a Watery one, and yet he gave Names to the several sorts of Fowls and Birds of the Air. Fowls, answered they, are partly Airy, and partly Earthly Creatures, not onely because they resemble Beasts and Men in their flesh, but because their rest and dwelling places are on Earth; for they build their Nests, lay their Eggs, and hatch their Young, not in the Air, but on the Earth. Then she asked, Whether the first Man did give Names to all the various sorts of Creatures that live on the Earth? Yes, answered they, to all those that were presented to him, or he had knowledg of, that is, to all the prime sorts; but not to every particular: for of Mankind, said they, there were but two at first; and as they did encrease, so did their Names. But, said the Empress, who gave the Names to the several sorts of Fish? The posterity of Mankind, answered they. Then she enquired, Whether there were no more kinds of Creatures now, then at the first Creation? They answered, That there were no more nor fewer kinds of Creatures then there are now; but there are, without question, more particular sorts of Creatures now, then there were then. she asked again, Whether all those Creatures that were in Paradise, were also in Noah's Ark? They answered, That the principal kinds had been there, but not all the particulars. Then she would fain know, how it came, that both Spirits and Men did fall from a blessed into so miserable a state and condition as they are now in. The Spirits answered, By disobedience. The Empress asked, Whence this disobedient sin did proceed? But the Spirits desired the Empress not to ask them any such questions, because they went beyond their knowledg. Then she begg'd the Spirits to pardon her presumption; for, said she, It is the nature of Mankind to be inquisitive. Natural desire of knowledg, answered the Spirits, is not blameable, so you do not go beyond what your Natural Reason can comprehend. Then I'le ask no more, said the Empress, for fear I should commit some error; but one thing I cannot but acquaint you withal: What is that, said the Spirits? I have a great desire, answered the Empress, to make a Cabbala. What kind of Cabbala asked the Spirits? The Empress answered, The Jews Cabbala. No sooner had the Empress declared her Mind, but the Spirits immediately disappeared out of her sight; which startled the Empress so much, that she fell into a Trance, wherein she lay for some while; at last being come to her self again, she grew very studious, and considering with her self what might be the cause of this strange dysaster, conceived at first, that perhaps the Spirits were tired with hearing and giving answers to her Questions; but thinking by her self, That Spirits could not be tired, she imagined that this was not the true cause of their disappearing, till, after divers debates with her own thoughts, she did verily believe that the Spirits had committed some fault in their answers, and that for their punishment they were condemned to the lowest and darkest Vehicles. This belief was so fixt in her mind, that it put her into a very Melancholick humor; and then she sent both for her Fly-men and Worm-men, and declared to them the cause of her sadness. 'Tis not so much, said she, the vanishing of those Spirits that makes me Melancholick, but that I should be the cause of their miserable condition, and that those harmless Spirits should, for my sake, sink down into the black and dark abyss of the Earth. The Worm-men comforted the Empress, telling her, That the Earth was not so horrid a Dwelling, as she did imagine; for, said they, not onely all Minerals and Vegetables, but several sorts of Animals can witness, that the Earth is a warm, fruitful, quiet, safe, and happy habitation; and though they want the light of the Sun, yet are they not in the dark, but there is light even within the Earth, by which those Creatures do see that dwell therein. This relation setled her Majesties mind a little; but yet she being desirous to know the Truth, where, and in what condition those Spirits were, commanded both the Fly- and Worm-men to use all labour and industry to find them out; whereupon the Worm-men straight descended into the Earth, and the Fly-men ascended into the Air. After some short time, the Worm-men returned, and told the Empress, that when they went into the Earth, they inquired of all the Creatures they met withal, Whether none of them had perceived such or such Spirits; until at last coming to the very Center of the Earth, they were truly informed, that those Spirits had stayed some time there, but at last were gone to the Antipodes on the other side of the Terrestrial Globe, diametrically opposite to theirs. The Fly-men seconded the Wormmen, assuring her Majesty, that their relation was very true; for, said they, We have rounded the Earth, and just when we came to the Antipodes, we met those Spirits in a very good condition, and acquainted them that your Majesty was very much troubled at their sudden departure, and fear'd they should be buried in the darkness of the Earth: whereupon the Spirits answered us, That they were sorry for having occasioned such sadness and trouble in your Majesty; and desired us to tell your Majesty, that they feared no darkness; for their Vehicles were of such a sort of substance as Cats eyes, Glow-worms tails, and rotten Wood, carrying their light along with them; and that they were ready to do your Majesty what service they could, in making your Cabbala. At which Relation the Empress was exceedingly glad, and rewarded both her Fly- and Worm-men bountifully.

After some time, when the Spirits had refreshed themselves in their own Vehicles, they sent one of their nimblest Spirits, to ask the Empress, Whether she would have a Scribe, or, whether she would write the Cabbala her self? The Empress received the proffer which they made her, with all civility; and told them, that she desired a Spiritual Scribe. The Spirits answer'd, That they could dictate, but not write, except they put on a hand or arm, or else the whole body of Man. The Empress replied, How can Spirits arm themselves with gantlets of Flesh? As well, answered they, as Man can arm himself with a gantlet of steel. If it be so, said the Empress, then I will have a Scribe. Then the Spirits asked her, Whether she would have the Soul of a living or a dead Man? Why, said the Empress, can the Soul quit a living Body, and wander or travel abroad? Yes, answered they, for according to Plato's Doctrine, there is a Conversation of Souls, and the Souls of Lovers live in the Bodies of their Beloved. Then I will have, answered she, the Soul of some ancient famous Writer, either of Aristotle, Pythagoras, Plato, Epicurus, or the like. The Spirits said, That those famous Men were very learned, subtile, and ingenious Writers; but they were so wedded to their own opinions, that they would never have the patience to be Scribes. Then, said she, I'le have the Soul of one of the most famous modern Writers, as either of Galileo, Gassendus, Des Cartes, Helmont, Hobbes, H. More, &c. The Spirits answered, That they were fine ingenious Writers, but yet so self-conceited, that they would scorn to be Scribes to a Woman. But, said they, there's a Lady, the Duchess of Newcastle; which although she is not one of the most learned, eloquent, witty and ingenious, yet she is a plain and rational Writer; for the principle of her Writings, is Sense and Reason, and she will without question, be ready to do you all the service she can. That Lady then, said the Empress, will I chuse for my Scribe, neither will the Emperor have reason to be jealous, she being one of my own sex. In truth, said the Spirit, Husbands have reason to be jealous of Platonick Lovers, for they are very dangerous, as being not onely intimate and close, but subtil and insinuating. You say well, replied the Empress; wherefore I pray send me the Duchess of Newcastle's Soul; which the Spirit did; and after she came to wait on the Empress, at her first arrival the Empress imbraced and saluted her with a Spiritual kiss; then she asked her whether she could write? Yes, answered the Duchess's Soul, but not so intelligibly that any Reader whatsoever may understand it, unless he be taught to know my Characters; for my Letters are rather like Characters, then well formed Letters. Said the Empress, you were recommended to me by an honest and ingenious Spirit. Surely, answered the Duchess, the Spirit is ignorant of my hand-writing. The truth is, said the Empress, he did not mention your hand-writing; but he informed me, that you writ Sense and Reason, and if you can but write so, that any of my Secretaries may learn your hand, they shall write it out fair and intelligible. The Duchess answered, That she questioned not but it might easily be learned in a short time. But, said she to the Empress, What is it that your Majesty would have written? she answered, The Jews Cabbala. Then your onely way for that is, said the Duchess, to have the Soul of some famous Jew; nay, if your Majesty please, I scruple not, but you may as easily have the Soul of Moses, as of any other. That cannot be, replied the Empress, for no Mortal knows where Moses is. But, said the Duchess, humane Souls are immortal; however, if this be too difficult to be obtained, you may have the Soul of one of the chief Rabbies or Sages of the Tribe of Levi, who will truly instruct you in that mystery; when as, otherwise, your Majesty will be apt to mistake, and a thousand to one, will commit gross errors. No, said the Empress, for I shall be instructed by Spirits. Alas! said the Duchess, Spirits are as ignorant as Mortals in many cases; for no created Spirits have a general or absolute knowledg, nor can they know the Thoughts of Men, much less the Mysteries of the great Creator, unless he be pleased to inspire into them the gift of Divine Knowledg. Then, I pray, said the Empress, let me have your counsel in this case. The Duchess answered, If your Majesty will be pleased to hearken to my advice, I would desire you to let that work alone; for it will be of no advantage either to you, or your people, unless you were of the Jews Religion; nay, if you were, the vulgar interpretation of the holy Scripture would be more instructive, and more easily believed, then your mystical way of interpreting it; for had it been better and more advantagious for the Salvation of the Jews, surely Moses would have saved after Ages that labour by his own Explanation, he being not onely a wise, but a very honest, zealous and religious Man: Wherefore the best way, said she, is to believe with the generality the literal sense of the Scripture, and not to make interpretations every one according to his own fancy, but to leave that work for the Learned, or those that have nothing else to do; Neither do I think, said she, that God will damn those that are ignorant therein, or suffer them to be lost for want of a Mystical interpretation of the Scripture. Then, said the Empress, I'le leave the Scripture, and make a Philosophical Cabbala. The Duchess told her, That, Sense and Reason would instruct her of a Nature as much as could be known; and as for Numbers, they were infinite; but to add non-sense to infinite, would breed a confusion, especially in Humane Understanding. Then, replied the Empress, I'le make a Moral Cabbala. The onely thing, answered the Duchess, in Morality, is but, To fear God, and to love his Neighbour, and this needs no further interpretation. But then I'le make a Political Cabbala, said the Empress. The Duchess answered, That the chief and onely ground in Government, was but Reward and Punishment, and required no further Cabbala; But, said she, If your Majesty were resolved to make a Cabbala, I would advise you, rather to make a Poetical or Romancical Cabbala, wherein you may use Metaphors, Allegories, Similitudes, &c. and interpret them as you please. With that the Empress thank'd the Duchess, and embracing her Soul, told her she would take her Counsel: she made her also her Favourite, and kept her sometime in that World, and by this means the Duchess came to know and give this Relation of all that passed in that rich, populous, and happy World; and after some time the Empress gave her leave to return to her Husband and Kindred into her Native World, but upon condition, that her Soul should visit her now and then; which she did: and truly their meeting did produce such an intimate friendship between them, that they became Platonick Lovers, although they were both Femals.

One time, when the Duchess her Soul was with the Empress, she seem'd to be very sad and melancholy; at which the Empress was very much troubled, and asked her the reason of her Melancholick humour? Truly, said the Duchess to the Empress, (for between dear friends there's no concealment, they being like several parts of one united body) my Melancholy proceeds from an extream Ambition. The Empress asked, What the height of her ambition was? The Duchess answered, That neither she her self, nor no Creature in the World was able to know either the height, depth, or breadth of her Ambition; but said she, my present desire is, that I would be a great Princess. The Empress replied, so you are; for you are a Princess of the fourth or fifth Degree, for a Duke or Duchess is the highest title or honour that a subject can arrive to, as being the next to a King's Title; and as for the name of a Prince of Princess, it belongs to all that are adopted to the Crown; so that those that can add a Crown to their Arms, are Princes, and therefore a Duke is a Title above a Prince; for example, the Duke of Savoy, the Duke of Florence, the Duke of Lorrain, as also Kings Brothers, are not called by the name of Princes, but Dukes, this being the higher Title. 'Tis true, answered the Duchess, unless it be Kings Eldest sons, and they are created Princes. Yes, replied the Empress, but no soveraign does make a subject equal to himself, such as Kings eldest sons partly are: And although some Dukes be soveraigns, yet I have heard that a Prince by his Title is soveraign, by reason the Title of a Prince is more a Title of Honour, then of soveraignty; for, as I said before, it belongs to all that are adopted to the Crown. Well, said the Duchess, setting aside this dispute, my Ambition is, That I would fain be as you are, that is, an Empress of a World, and I shall never be at quiet until I be one. I love you so well, replied the Empress, that I wish with all my soul, you had the fruition of your ambitious desire, and I shall not fail to give you my best advice how to accomplish it; the best informers are the Immaterial Spirits, and they'l soon tell you, Whether it be possible to obtain your wish. But, said the Duchess, I have little acquaintance with them, for I never knew any before the time you sent for me. They know you, replied the Empress; for they told me of you, and were the means and instrument of your coming hither: Wherefore I'le conferr with them, and enquire whether there be not another World, whereof you may be Empress as well as I am of this? No sooner had the Empress said this, but some Immaterial Spirits came to visit her, of whom she inquired, Whether there were but three Worlds in all, to wit, the Blazing World where she was in, the World which she came from, and the World where the Duchess lived? The Spirits answered, That there were more numerous Worlds then the Stars which appeared in these three mentioned Worlds. Then the Empress asked, Whether it was not possible that her dearest friend the Duchess of Newcastle, might be Empress of one of them? Although there be numerous, nay, infinite Worlds, answered the Spirits, yet none is without Government. But is none of these Worlds so weak, said she, that it may be surprized or conquered? The Spirits answered, That Lucian's World of Lights, had been for some time in a snuff, but of late years one Helmont had got it, who since he was Emperour of it, had so strengthened the Immortal parts thereof with mortal out-works, as it was for the present impregnable. said the Empress, If there be such an Infinite number of Worlds, I am sure, not onely my friend, the Duchess, but any other might obtain one. Yes, answered the Spirits, if those Worlds were uninhabited; but they are as populous as this your Majesty governs. Why, said the Empress, it is not possible to conquer a World. No, answered the Spirits, but, for the most part, Conquerers seldom enjoy their conquest, for they being more feared then loved, most commonly come to an untimely end. If you will but direct me, said the Duchess to the Spirits, which World is easiest to be conquered, her Majesty will assist me with Means, and I will trust to Fate and Fortune; for I had rather die in the adventure of noble atchievements, then live in obscure and sluggish security; since the by one, I may live in a glorious Fame; and by the other I am buried in oblivion. The Spirits answered, That the lives of Fame were like other lives; for some lasted long, and some died soon. 'Tis true, said the Duchess; but yet the shortest-liv'd Fame lasts longer then the longest life of Man. But, replied the Spirits, if occasion does not serve you, you must content your self to live without such atchievements that may gain you a Fame: But we wonder, proceeded the Spirits, that you desire to be Empress of a Terrestrial World, when as you can create your self a Cœlestial World if you please. What, said the Empress, can any Mortal be a Creator? Yes, answered the Spirits; for every human Creature can create an Immaterial World fully inhabited by Immaterial Creatures, and populous of Immaterial subjects, such as we are, and all this within the compass of the head or scull; nay, not onely so, but he may create a World of what fashion and Government he will, and give the Creatures thereof such motions, figures, forms, colours, perceptions, &c. as he pleases, and make Whirl-pools, Lights, Pressures, and Reactions, &c. as he thinks best; nay, he may make a World full of Veins, Muscles, and Nerves, and all these to move by one jolt or stroke: also he may alter that World as often as he pleases, or change it from a Natural World, to an Artificial; he may make a World of Ideas, a World of Atoms, a World of Lights, or whatsoever his Fancy leads him to. And since it is in your power to create such a World, What need you to venture life, reputation and tranquility, to conquer a gross material World? For you can enjoy no more of a material world then a particular Creature is able to enjoy, which is but a small part, considering the compass of such a world; and you may plainly observe it by your friend the Empress here, which although she possesses a whole World, yet enjoys she but a part thereof; neither is she so much acquainted with it, that she know all the places, Countries, and Dominions she Governs. The truth is, a soveraign Monarch has the general trouble; but the Subjects enjoy all the delights and pleasures in parts, for it is impossible, that a Kingdom, nay, a Country, should be injoyed by one person at once, except he take the pains to travel into every part, and endure the inconveniencies of going from one place to another? wherefore, since glory, delight, and pleasure lives but in other mens opinions, and can neither add tranquility to your mind nor give ease to your body, Why should you desire to be Empress of a Material World, and be troubled with the cares that attend Government? when as by creating a World within your self, you may enjoy all both in whole and in parts, without controle or opposition; and may make what World you please, and alter it when you please, and enjoy as much pleasure and delight as a World can afford you? You have converted me, said the Duchess to the Spirits, from my ambitious desire; wherefore, I'le take your advice, reject and despise all the Worlds without me, and create a World of my own. The Empress said, If I do make such a world, then I shall be Mistress of two Worlds, one within, and the other without me. That your Majesty may, said the Spirits; and so left these two Ladies to create two Worlds within themselves: who did also part from each other, until such time as they had brought their Worlds to perfection. The Duchess of Newcastle was most earnest and industrious to make her World, because she had none at present; and first she resolved to frame it according to the opinion of Thales, but she found her self so much troubled with Dæmons, that they would not suffer her to take her own will, but forced her to obey their orders and commands; which she being unwilling to do, left off from making a world that way, and began to frame one according to Pythagoras's Doctrine; but in the Creation thereof, she was so puzled with numbers, how to order and compose the several parts, that she having no skill in Arithmetick, was forced also to desist from the making of that World. Then she intended to create a World according to the opinion of Plato; but she found more trouble and difficulty in that, then in the two former; for the numerous Idea's having no other motion but what was derived from her mind, whence they did flow and issue out, made it a far harder business to her, to impart motion to them, then Puppit-players have in giving motion to every several Puppit; in so much, that her patience was not able to endure the trouble which those Ideas caused her; wherefore she annihilated also that World, and was resolved to make one according to the Opinion of Epicurus; which she had no sooner begun, but the infinite Atoms made such a mist, that it quite blinded the perception of her mind; neither was she able to make a Vacuum as a receptacle for those Atoms, or a place which they might retire into; so that partly for the want of it, and of a good order and method, the confusion of those Atoms produced such strange and monstrous figures, as did more affright then delight her, and caused such a Chaos in her mind, as had almost dissolved it. At last, having with much ado cleansed and cleared her mind of these dusty and misty particles, she endeavored to create a World according to Aristotle's Opinion; but remembring that her mind, as most of the Learned hold it, was Immaterial, and that, according to Aristotle's Principle, out of Nothing, Nothing could be made; she was forced also to desist from that work, and then she fully resolved, not to take any more patterns from the Ancient Philosophers, but to follow the Opinions of the Moderns; and to that end, she endeavoured to make a World according to Des Cartes Opinion; but when she had made the Æthereal Globules, and set them a moving by a strong and lively imagination, her mind became so dizzie with their extraordinary swift turning round, that it almost put her into a swoon; for her thoughts, but their constant tottering, did so stagger, as if they had all been drunk: wherefore she dissolved that World, and began to make another, according to Hobbs's Opinion; but when all the parts of this Imaginary World came to press and drive each other, they seemed like a company of Wolves that worry sheep, or like so many Dogs that hunt after Hares; and when she found a re-action equal to those pressures, her mind was so squeezed together, that her thoughts could neither move forward nor backward, which caused such an horrible pain in her head, that although she had dissolved that World, yet she could not, without much difficulty, settle her mind, and free it from that pain which those pressures and reactions had caused in it.

 At last, when the Duchess saw that no patterns would do her any good in the framing of her World; she was resolved to make a World of her own Invention, and this World was composed of sensitive and rational self-moving Matter; indeed, it was composed onely of the Rational, which is the subtilest and purest degree of Matter; for as the Sensitive did move and act both to the perceptions and consistency of the body, so this degree of Matter at the same point of time (for though the degrees are mixt, yet the several parts may move several ways at one time) did move to the Creation of the Imaginary World; which World after it was made, appear'd so curious and full of variety, so well order'd and wisely govern'd, that it cannot possibly be expressed by words, nor the delight and pleasure which the Duchess took in making this World-of-her-own.

In the mean time the Empress was also making and dissolving several Worlds in her own mind, and was so puzled, that she could not settle in any of them; wherefore she sent for the Duchess, who being ready to wait on the Empress, carried her beloved World along with her, and invited the Empress's Soul to observe the Frame, Order and Government of it. Her Majesty was so ravished with the perception of it, that her Soul desired to live in the Duchess's World: But the Duchess advised her to make such another World in her own mind; for, said she, your Majesty's mind is full of rational corporeal motions; and the rational motions of my mind shall assist you by the help of sensitive expressions, with the best Instructions they are able to give you.

The Empress being thus perswaded by the Duchess to make an imaginary World of her own, followed her advice; and after she had quite finished it, and framed all kinds of Creatures proper and useful for it, strengthened it with good Laws, and beautified it with Arts and Sciences; having nothing else to do, unless she did dissolve her Imaginary World, or made some alterations in the Blazing-World, she lived in; which yet she could hardly do, by reason it was so well ordered that it could not be mended; for it was governed without secret and deceiving Policy; neither was there any ambitious, factions, malicious detractions, civil dissentions, or home-bred quarrels, divisions in Religion, Foreign Wars, &c. but all the people lived in a peaceful society, united Tranquility, and Religious Conformity. she was desirious to see the World the Duchess came from, and observe therein the several sovereign Governments, Laws and Customs of several Nations. The Duchess used all the means she could, to divert her from that Journey, telling her, that the World she came from, was very much disturbed with Factions, Divisions and Wars; but the Empress would not be perswaded from her design; and lest the Emperor, or any of his subjects should know of her travel, and obstruct her design;

she sent for some of the Spirits she had formerly conversed withal, and inquired whether none of them could supply the place of her soul in her body at such a time, when she was gone to travel into another World? They answered, Yes, they could; for not onely one, said they, but many Spirits may enter into your body, if you please. The Empress replied, she desired but one Spirit to be Vice-Roy of her body in the absence of her Soul, but it must be an honest and ingenious Spirit; and if it was possible, a female Spirit. The Spirits told her, that there was no difference of Sexes amongst them; but, said they, we will chuse an honest and ingenious Spirit, and such a one as shall so resemble your soul, that neither the Emperor, nor any of his Subjects, although the most Divine, shall know whether it be your own soul, or not: which the Empress was very glad at, and after the Spirits were gone, asked the Duchess, how her body was supplied in the absence of her soul? who answered Her Majesty, That her body, in the absence of her soul, was governed by her sensitive and rational corporeal motions. Thus those two Female Souls travelled together as lightly as two thoughts into the Duchess her native World; and, which is remarkable, in a moment viewed all the parts of it, and all the actions of all the Creatures therein, especially did the Empress's Soul take much notice of the several actions of humane Creatures in all the several Nations and parts of that World, and wonder'd that for all there were so many several Nations, Governments, Laws, Religions, Opinions, &c. they should all yet so generally agree in being Ambitious, Proud, Self-conceited, Vain, Prodigal, Deceitful, Envious, Malicious, Unjust, Revengeful, Irreligious, Factious, &c. she did also admire, that not any particular State, Kingdom or Common-wealth, was contented with their own shares, but endeavoured to encroach upon their Neighbours, and that their greatest glory was in Plunder and Slaughter, and yet their victory's less then their expences, and their losses more than their gains; but their being overcome, in a manner their utter ruine: But that she wonder'd most at, was, that they should prize or value dirt more then mens lives, and vanity more then tranquility: for the Emperor of a world, said she, injoys but a part, not the whole; so that his pleasure consists in the Opinions of others. It is strange to me, answered the Duchess, that you should say thus, being your self, an Empress of a World; and not onely of a world, but of a peaceable, quiet, and obedient world. 'Tis true, replied the Empress: but although it is a peaceable and obedient world, yet the Government thereof is rather a trouble, then a pleasure; for order cannot be without industry, contrivance, and direction: besides, the Magnificent state, that great Princes keep or ought to keep, is troublesome. Then by your Majestie's discourse, said the Duchess, I perceive that the greatest happiness in all the Worlds consist in Moderation: No doubt of it, replied the Empress; and after these two souls had visited all the several places, Congregations and Assemblies both in Religion and State, the several Courts of Judicature and the like, in several Nations, the Empress said, That of all the Monarchs of the several parts of the World, she had observed the Grand-Seignior was the greatest; for his word was a Law, and his power absolute. But the Duchess pray'd the Empress to pardon her that she was of another mind; for, said she, he cannot alter Mahomets Laws and Religion; so that the Law and Church do govern the Emperor, and not the Emperor them. But, replied the Empress, he has power in some particulars; as for example, To place and displace Subjects in their particular Governments of Church and State; and having that, he has the Command both over Church and State, and none dares oppose him. 'Tis true, said the Duchess; but if it pleases your Majesty, we will go into that part of the World whence I came to wait on your Majesty, and there you shall see as powerful a Monarch as the Grand Signior; for though his Dominions are not of so large extent, yet they are much stronger, his Laws are easie and safe, and he governs so justly and wisely, that his Subjects are the happiest people of all the Nations or parts of that World. This Monarch, said the Empress, I have a great mind to see. Then they both went, and in a short time arrived into his Dominions; but coming into the Metropolitan City, the Empress's Soul observed many Gallants go into an House; and enquiring of the Duchess's Soul, what House that was? she told her, It was one of the Theatres where Comedies and Tragedies were acted. The Empress asked, Whether they were real? No, said the Duchess, they are feigned. Then the Empress desired to enter into the Theatre; and when she had seen the Play that was asked, the Duchess asked her how she liked that Recreation? I like it very well, said the Empress; but I observe that the Actors make a better show than the Spectators; and the Scenes a better than the Actors and the Musick and Dancing is more pleasant and acceptable than the Play it self; for I see, the Scenes stand for Wit, the Dancing for Humour, and the Musick is the Chorus. I am sorry, replied the Duchess, to hear your Majesty say so; for if the Wits of this part of the

World should hear you, they would condemn you. What, said the Empress, would they condemn me for preferring a natural Face before a Sign-post; or a natural Humour before an artificial Dance; or Musick before a true and profitable Relation? As for Relation, replied the Duchess, our Poets defie and condemn it into a Chimney-corner, fitter for old Womens Tales, than Theatres. Why, said the Empress do not your Poets Actions comply with their Judgments? For their Plays are composed of old Stories, either of Greek or Roman, or some new-found World. The Duchess answered Her Majesty, That it was true, that all or most of their Plays were taken out of old Stories; but yet they had new Actions, which being joined to old Stories, together with the addition of new Prologues, Scenes, Musick and Dancing, made new Plays.

After this, both the Souls went to the Court, where all the Royal Family was together, attended by the chief of the Nobles of their Dominions, which made a very magnificent Show; and when the Soul of the Empress viewed the King and Queen, she seemed to be in a maze, which the Duchess's Soul perceiving, asked the Empress how she liked the King, the Queen, and all the Royal Race? she answered, that in all the Monarchs she had seen in that World, she had not found so much Majesty and Affability mixt so exactly together, that none did overshadow or eclipse the other; and as for the Queen, she said that Vertue sat Triumphant in her face, and Piety was dwelling in her heart; and that all the Royal Family seem'd to be endued with a Divine splendor: but when she had heard the King discourse, she believ'd that Mercury and Apollo had been his Cœlestial Instructors; and, my dear Lord and Husband, added the Duchess, has been his Earthly Governor. But after some short stay in the Court, the Duchess's soul grew very Melancholy; the Empress asking the cause of her sadness? she told her, That she had an extreme desire to converse with the soul of her Noble Lord and dear Husband, and that she was inpatient of a longer stay. The Empress desired the Duchess to have but patience so long, until the King, the Queen, and the Royal Family were retired, and then she would bear her Company to her Lord and Husband's Soul, who at that time lived in the Country some 112 miles off; which she did: and thus these two souls went towards those parts of the Kingdom where the Duke of Newcastle was.

But one thing I forgot all this while, which is, That although thoughts are the natural language of Souls; yet by reason Souls cannot travel without Vehicles, they use such language as the nature and propriety of their Vehicles require, and the Vehicles of those two souls being made of the purest and finest sort of air, and of a human shape: This purity and fineness was the cause that they could neither be seen nor heard by any human Creature; when as, had they been of some grosser sort of Air, the sound of the Air's language would have been as perceptible as the blowing of Zephyrus.

And now to return to my former Story; when the Empress's and Duchess's Soul were travelling into Nottinghamshire, (for that was the place where the Duke did reside) passing through the Forrest of sherewood, the Empress's Soul was very much delighted with it, as being a dry, plain and woody place, very pleasant to travel in, both in Winter and Summer; for it is neither much dirty nor dusty at no time: At last they arrived at Welbeck, a House where the Duke dwell'd, surrounded all with Wood, so close and full, that the Empress took great pleasure and delight therein, and told the Duchess she never had observed more Wood in so little compass in any part of the Kingdom she had passed through. The truth is, said she, there seems to be more Wood on the Seas (she meaning the Ships) than on the Land. The Duchess told her, The reason was, that there had been a long Civil Warr in that Kingdom, in which most of the best Timber-trees and Principal Palaces were ruined and destroyed; and my dear Lord and Husband, said she, has lost by it half his Woods, besides many Houses, Land, and movable Goods; so that all the loss out of his particular Estate, did amount to above Half a Million of Pounds. I wish, said the Empress, he had some of the Gold that is in the Blazing-World, to repair his losses. The Duchess most humbly thank'd her Imperial Majesty for her kind wishes; but, said she, Wishes will not repair his ruins: however, God has given my Noble Lord and Husband great Patience, by which he bears all his losses and misfortunes. As last they enter'd into the Duke's House, an Habitation not so magnificent as useful; and when the Empress saw it, Has the Duke, said she, no other House but this? Yes, answered the Duchess, some five miles from this place he has a very fine Castle called Bolesover. That place, then, said the Empress, I desire to see. Alas, replied the Duchess, it is but a naked House, and uncloath'd of all Furniture. However, said the Empress, I may see the manner of its structure and building. That you may, replied the Duchess, and as they were thus discoursing, the Duke came out of the House into the Court, to see his Horses of Manage; whom when the Duchess's Soul perceived, she was so overjoyed, that her Aereal Vehicle became so splendorous, as if it had been enlightned by the Sun; by which we may perceive, that the passions of Souls or Spirits can alter their bodily Vehicles. Then these two Ladies Spirits went close to him, but he could not perceive them; and after the Empress had observed that Art of Mannage, she was much pleased with it, and commended it as a noble pastime, and an exercise fit and proper for noble and heroick Persons. But when the Duke was gone into the house again, those two Souls followed him; where the Empress observing, that he went to the exercise of the sword, and was such an excellent and unparallel'd Master thereof, she was as much pleased with that exercise, as she was with the former: But the Duchess's Soul being troubled, that her dear Lord and Husband used such a violent exercise before meat, for fear of overheating himself, without any consideration of the Empress's Soul, left her Æreal Vehicle, and entred into her Lord. The Empress's Soul perceiving this, did the like: And then the Duke had three Souls in one Body; and had there been some such Souls more, the Duke would have been like the Grand-Signior in his Seraglio, onely it would have been a Platonick Seraglio. But the Duke's Soul being wise, honest, witty, complaisant and noble, afforded such delight and pleasure to the Empress's Soul by his conversation, that these two souls became enamoured of each other; which the Duchess's soul perceiving, grew jealous at first, but then considering that no Adultery could be committed amongst Platonick Lovers, and that Platonism, was Divine, as being derived from Divine Plato, cast forth of her mind that Idea of Jealousie. Then the Conversation of these three souls was so pleasant, that it cannot be expressed; for the Duke's Soul entertained the Empress's Soul with Scenes, songs, Musick, witty Discourses, pleasant Recreations, and all kinds of harmless sports, so that the time passed away faster than they expected. At last a Spirit came and told the Empress, That although neither the Emperor nor any of his Subjects knew that her Soul was absent; yet the Emperor's Soul was so sad and melancholy for want of His own beloved Soul, that all the Imperial Court took notice of it. Wherefore he advised the Empress's Soul to return into the Blazing-World, into her own Body she left there; which both the Duke's and Duchess's Soul was very sorry for, and wished that, if it had been possible, the Empress's Soul might have stayed a longer time with them;

but seeing it could not be otherwise, they pacified themselves. But before the Empress returned into the Blazing-World, the Duchess desired a Favour of her, to wit, That she would be pleased to make an Agreement between her Noble Lord, and Fortune. Why, said the Empress, are they Enemies? Yes, answered the Duchess, and they have been so ever since I have been his Wife: nay, I have heard my Lord say, That she hath crossed him in all things, ever since he could remember. I am sorry for that, replied the Empress; but I cannot discourse with Fortune, without the help of an Immaterial Spirit, and that cannot be done in this World; for I have no Fly nor Bird-men here, to send into the Region of the Air, where, for the most part, their Habitations are. The Duchess said, she would entreat her Lord to send an Attorney or Lawyer to plead his Cause. Fortune will bribe them, replied the Empress, and so the Duke may chance to be cast: Wherefore the best way will be, for the Duke to chuse a Friend on his side, and let Fortune chuse another, and try whether by this means it be possible to compose the Difference. The Duchess said, They will never come to an agreement, unless there be a Judg or Umpire to decide the Case. A Judg, replied the Empress, is easie to be had; but to get an Impartial Judg, is a thing so difficult, that I doubt we shall hardly find one; for there is none to be had, neither in Nature, nor in Hell, but onely from Heaven; and how to get such a Divine and Celestial Judg, I cannot tell: Nevertheless, if you will go along with me into the Blazing-World, I'le try what may be done. 'Tis my duty, said the Duchess, to wait on your Majesty, and I shall most willingly do it, for I have no other interest to consider. Then the Duchess spake to the Duke concerning the difference between him and Fortune, and how it was her desire that they might be friends. The Duke answered, That for his part he had always with great industry sought her friendship, but as yet he could never obtain it, for she had always been his Enemy. However, said he, I'le try and send my two Friends, Prudence and Honesty, to plead my Cause. Then these two Friends went with the Duchess and the Empress into the Blazing-World; (for it is to be observed, that they are somewhat like Spirits, because they are Immaterial, although their actions are corporeal:) and after their arrival there, when the Empress had refreshed her self, and rejoiced with the Emperor, she sent her Fly-men for some of the Spirits, and desired their assistance, to compose the difference between Fortune, and the Duke of Newcastle. But they told her Majesty, That Fortune was so inconstant, that although she would perhaps promise to hear their Cause pleaded, yet it was a thousand to one, whether she would ever have the patience to do it: Nevertheless, upon Her Majestie's request, they tried their utmost, and at last prevailed with Fortune so far, that she chose Folly and Rashness, for her Friends, but they could not agree in chusing a Judg; until at last, with much ado, they concluded, that Truth should hear, and decide the cause. Thus all being prepared, and the time appointed, both the Empress and Duchess's Soul went to hear them plead; and when all the Immaterial Company was met, Fortune standing upon a Golden-Globe, made this following Speech:

Noble Friends, We are met here to hear a Cause pleaded concerning the difference between the Duke of Newcastle, and my self; and though I am willing upon the perswasions of the Ambassadors of the Empress, the Immaterial Spirits, to yield to it, yet it had been fit, the Duke's Soul should be present also, to speak for her self; but since she is not here, I shall declare my self to his Wife, and his Friends, as also to my Friends, especially the Empress, to whom I shall chiefly direct my Speech. First, I desire your Imperial Majesty may know, that this Duke who complains or exclaims so much against me, hath been always my enemy; for he has preferred Honesty and Prudence before me, and slighted all my favours; nay, not onely thus, but he did fight against me, and preferred his Innocence before my Power. His Friends Honesty and Prudence, said he most scornfully, are more to be regarded, than Inconstant Fortune, who is onely a friend to Fools and Knaves; for which neglect and scorn, whether I have not just reason to be his enemy, your Majesty may judg your self.

After Fortune had thus ended her Speech, the Duchess's Soul rose from her seat, and spake to the Immaterial Assembly in this manner:

Noble Friends, I think it fit, by your leave, to answer Lady Fortune in the behalf of my Noble Lord and Husband, since he is not here himself; and since you have heard her complaint concerning the choice my Lord made of his Friends, and the neglect and disrespect he seemed to cast upon her; give me leave to answer, that, first concerning the Choice of his Friends, He has proved himself a wise man in it; and as for the disrespect and rudeness her Ladiship accuses him of, I dare say he is so much a Gentleman, that I am confident he would never slight, scorn or disrespect any of the Female Sex in all his life time; but was such a servant and Champion for them, that he ventured Life and Estate in their service; but being of an honest, as well as an honourable Nature, he could not trust Fortune with that which he preferred above his life, which was his Reputation, by reason Fortune did not side with those that were honest and honourable, but renounced them; and since he could not be of both sides, he chose to be of that which was agreeable both to his Conscience, Nature and Education; for which choice Fortune did not onely declare her self his open Enemy, but fought with him in several Battels; nay, many times, hand to hand; at last, she being a Powerful Princess, and as some believe, a Deity, overcame him, and cast him into a Banishment, where she kept him in great misery, ruined his Estate, and took away from him most of his Friends; nay, even when she favoured many that were against her, she still frowned on him; all which he endured with the greatest patience, and with that respect to Lady Fortune, that he did never in the least endeavour to disoblige any of her Favourites, but was onely sorry that he, an honest man, could find no favor in her Court; and since he did never injure any of those she favoured, he neither was an enemy to her Ladiship, but gave her always that respect and worship which belonged to her power and dignity, and is still ready at any time honestly and prudently to serve her; he onely begs, her Ladiship would be his friend for the future, as she hath been his enemy in times past.

As soon as the Duchess's Speech was ended, Folly and Rashness started up, and both spake so thick and fast at once, that not onely the Assembly, but themselves were not able to understand each other: At which Fortune was somewhat out of countenance; and commanded them either to speak singly, or be silent: But Prudence told her Ladiship, she should command them to speak wisely, as well as singly; otherwise, said she, it were best for them not to speak at all: Which Fortune resented very ill, and told Prudence, she was too bold; and then commanded Folly to declare what she would have made known: but her Speech was so foolish, mixt with such Non-sense, that none knew what to make of it; besides, it was so tedious, that Fortune bid her to be silent; and commanded Rashness to speak for her, who began after this manner:

Great Fortune; The Duchess of Newcastle has proved her self, according to report, a very Proud and Ambitious Lady, in presuming to answer you her own self, in this noble Assembly without your Command, in a Speech wherein she did not onely contradict you, but preferred Honesty and Prudence before you; saying, That her Lord was ready to serve you honestly and prudently; which presumption is beyond all pardon; and if you allow Honesty and Prudence to be above you, none will admire, worship, or serve you; but you'l be forced to serve your self, and will be despised, neglected and scorned by all; and from a Deity, become a miserable, dirty, begging mortal in a Church-yard-Porch, or Noble-man's Gate: Wherefore to prevent such disasters, fling as many misfortunes and neglects on the Duke and Duchess of Newcastle, and their two friends, as your power is able to do; otherwise Prudence and Honesty will be the chief and onely Moral Deities of Mortals.

Rashness having thus ended her Speech, Prudence rose and declared her self in this manner:

Beautiful Truth, Great Fortune, and you the rest of my noble Friends; I am come a great and long journey in the behalf of my dear Friend the Duke of Newcastle; not to make more wounds, but, if it be possible, to heal those that are made already. Neither do I presume to be a Deity; but my onely request is, that you would be pleased to accept of my Offering, I being an humble and devout supplicant; and since no offering is more acceptable to the Gods, then the offering of Peace; in order to that, I desire to make an agreement between Fortune, and the Duke of Newcastle.

Thus she spake, and as she was going up, up started Honesty (for she has not always so much discretion as she ought to have) and interrupted Prudence.

I came not here, said she, to hear Fortune flattered, but to hear the Cause decided between Fortune and the Duke; neither came I hither to speak Rhetorically and Eloquently, but to propound the case plainly and truly; and I'le have you know, that the Duke, whose Cause we argue, was and is my Foster-son; for I Honesty bred him from his Childhood, and made a perpetual friendship betwixt him and Gratitude, Charity and Generosity; and put him to School to Prudence, who taught him Wisdom, and informed him in the Rules of Temperance, Patience, Justice, and the like; then I put him into the University of Honour, where he learned all Honourable Qualities, Arts, and Sciences; afterward I sent him to travel through the World of Actions, and made Observation his Governor; and in those his travels, he contracted a friendship with Experience; all which, made him fit for Heavens Blessings, and Fortunes Favours: But she hating all those that have merit and desert, became his inveterate Enemy, doing him all the mischief she could, until the God of Justice opposed Fortune's

Malice, and pull'd him out of those ruines she had cast upon him: For this God's Favourites were the Dukes Champions; wherefore to be an Enemy to him, were to be an Enemy to the God of Justice: In short, the true cause of Fortunes Malice to this Duke is, that he would never flatter her; for I Honesty, did command him not to do it, or else he would be forced to follow all her inconstant ways, and obey all her unjust commands, which would cause a great reproach to him: but, on the other side, Prudence advised him not to despise Fortune's favours, for that would be an obstrustion and hinderance to his worth and merit; and He to obey both our advice and counsels, did neither flatter nor despise Her; but was always humble and respectful to her so far as Honour, Honesty and Conscience would permit: all which I refer to Truth's Judgment, and expect her final Sentence.

Fortune hearing thus Honesty's plain Speech, thought it very rude, and would not hearken to Truth's Judgment, but went away in a Passion: At which, both the Empress and Duchess were extreamly troubled, that their endeavours should have no better effect: but Honesty chid the Duchess, and said, she was to be punished for desiring so much Fortune's favours; for it appears, said she, that you mistrust the gods blessings: At which the Duchess wept, answering Honesty, That she did neither mistrust the gods blessings, nor relye upon Fortune's favours; but desired onely that her Lord might have no potent Enemies. The Empress being much troubled to see her weep, told Honesty in anger, she wanted the discretion of Prudence; for though you are commended, said she, yet you are apt to commit many indiscreet actions, unless Prudence be your guide. At which reproof Prudence smiled, and Honesty was somewhat out of countenance; but they soon became very good friends: and after the Duchess's Soul had stayed some time with the Empress in the Blazing-World, she begg'd leave of her to return to her Lord and Husband; which the Empress granted her, upon condition she should come and visit her as often as conveniently she could, promising that she would do the same to the Duchess.

Thus the Duchess's soul, after she had taken her leave of the Empress, as also of the Spirits, who with great civility, promised her, that they would endeavour in time to make a Peace and Agreement between Fortune and the Duke, returned with Prudence and Honesty, into her own World: But when she was just upon her departure, the Empress sent to

Her, and desired that she might yet have some little conference with her before she went; which the Duchess most willingly granted her Majesty; and when she came to wait on her, the Empress told the Duchess, That she being her dear Platonick Friend, of whose just and Impartial Judgment, she had alwayes a very great esteem; could not forbear, before she went from her, to ask her Advice concerning the Government of the Blazing-World: For, said she, although this World was very well and wisely ordered and governed at first, when I came to be Empress thereof; yet the nature of Women being much delighted with Change and Variety, after I had received an absolute Power from the Emperor, did somewhat alter the Form of Government from what I found it; but now perceiving that the World is not so quiet as it was at first, I am much troubled at it; especially there are such continual Contentions and Divisions between the Worm- Bear- and Fly-men, the Ape-men, the Satyrs, the Spider-men, and all others of such sorts, that I fear they'l break out into an open Rebellion, and cause a great disorder; and the ruin of the Government; and therefore I desire your advice and assistance, how I may order it to the best advantage, that this World may be rendred peaceable, quiet and happy, as it was before. Whereupon the Duchess answered, That since she heard by her Imperial Majesty, how well and happily the World had been governed when she first came to be Empress thereof, she would advise her Majesty to introduce the same form of Government again, which had been before; that is, to have but one soveraign, one Religion, one Law, and one Language, so that all the World might be but as one united Family, without divisions; nay, like God, and his Blessed Saints and Angels: Otherwise, said she, it may in time prove as unhappy, nay, as miserable a World as that is from which I came, wherein are more soveraigns then Worlds, and more pretended Governours then Government, more Religions then Gods, and more Opinions in those Religions then Truths; more Laws then Rights, and more Bribes then Justices; more Policies then Necessities, and more Fears then Dangers; more Covetousness then Riches, more Ambitions then Merits, more Services then Rewards, more Languages then Wit, more Controversie then Knowledg, more Reports then noble Actions, and more Gifts by partiality, then according to Merit; all which, said she, is a great misery, nay, a curse, which your blessed Blazing-World never knew, nor 'tis probable, will never know of, unless your Imperial Majesty alter the Government thereof from what it was when you began to govern it: And since your Majesty complains much of the factions of the Bear- Fish- Fly- Ape- and Worm-men, the Satyrs, Spider-men, and the like, and of their perpetual disputes and quarrels, I would advise your Majesty to dissolve all their societies; for 'tis better to be without their intelligences, then to have an unquiet and disorderly Government. The truth is, said she, wheresoever Learning is, there is most commonly also Controversie and quarelling; for there be always some that will know more, and be wiser then others: some think their Arguments come nearer to Truth, and are more rational then others; some are so wedded to their own opinions, that they'l never yield to Reason; and others, though they find their Opinions not firmly grounded upon Reason, yet, for fear of receiving some disgrace by altering them, will nevertheless maintain them against all sense and reason, which must needs breed factions in their Schools, which at last break out into open Wars, and draw sometimes an utter ruin upon a State or Government. The Empress told the Duchess, that she would willingly follow her advice; but she thought it would be an eternal disgrace to her, to alter her own Decrees, Acts, and Laws. To which the Duchess answered, That it was so far from a disgrace, as it would rather be for her Majesties eternal honour, to return from a worse to a better, and would express and declare Her to be more then ordinary wise and good; so wise, as to perceive her own errors, and so good, as not to persist in them, which few did: for which, said she, you will get a glorious fame in this World, and an Eternal Glory hereafter; and I shall pray for it so long as I live. Upon which Advice, the Empress's Soul embrac'd and kiss'd the Duchess's Soul with an Immaterial Kiss, and shed Immaterial Tears, that she was forced to part from her, finding her not a flattering Parasite, but a true Friend; and in truth, such was their Platonick Friendship, as these two loving Souls did often meet and rejoice in each others Conversation.

# The Second Part of the Description of the New Blazing-World.

The Empress having now ordered and setled her Government to the best advantage and quiet of her Blazing-World, lived and reigned most happily and blessedly, and received oftentimes Visits from the Immaterial Spirits, who gave her Intelligence of all such things as she desired to know, and they were able to inform her of: One time they told her, how the World she came from, was imbroiled in a great War, and that most parts or Nations thereof made War against that Kingdom which was her Native Country, where all her Friends and Relations did live; at which the Empress was extreamly troubled; insomuch that the Emperor perceived her grief by her tears, and examining the cause thereof, she told him that she had received Intelligence from the Spirits, that that part of the World she came from, which was her native Country, was like to be destroyed by numerous Enemies that made War against it. The Emperor being very sensible of this ill news, especially of the Trouble it caused to the Empress, endeavoured to comfort her as much as possibly he could; and told her, that she might have all the assistance which the Blazing-World was able to afford. she answered, That if there were any possibility of transporting Forces out of the Blazing-World, into the World she came from, she would not fear so much the ruin thereof: but, said she, there being no probability of effecting anysuch thing, I know not how to shew my readiness to serve my Native Country. The Emperor asked, Whether those Spirits that gave her Intelligence of this War, could not with all their Power and Forces, assist her against those Enemies? she answered, That Spirits could not arm themselves, nor make any use of Artificial Arms or Weapons; for their Vehicles were Natural Bodies, not Artificial: Besides, said she, the violent and strong actions of war, will never agree with Immaterial Spirits; for Immaterial Spirits cannot fight, nor make Trenches, Fortifications, and the like. But, said the Emperor, their Vehicles can; especially if those Vehicles be mens Bodies, they may be serviceable in all the actions of War. Alas, replied the Empress, that will never do; for first, said she, it will be difficult to get so many dead Bodies for their Vehicles, as to make up a whole Army, much more to make many Armies to fight with so many several Nations; nay, if this could be, yet it is not possible to get so many dead and undissolved Bodies in one Nation; and for transporting them out of other Nations, it would be a thing of great difficulty and improbability: But put the case, said she, all these difficulties could be overcome; yet there is one obstruction or hindrance which can no ways be avoided: For although those dead and undissolved Bodies did all die in one minute of time; yet before they could Rendezvouze, and be put into a posture of War, to make a great and formidable Army, they would stink and dissolve; and when they came to a fight, they would moulder into dust and ashes, and so leave the purer Immaterial Spirits naked: nay, were it also possible, that those dead bodies could be preserved from stinking and dissolving, yet the Souls of such Bodies would not suffer Immaterial Spirits to rule and order them, but they would enter and govern them themselves, as being the right owners thereof, which would produce a War between those Immaterial Souls, and the Immaterial Spirits in Material Bodies; all which would hinder them from doing any service in the actions of War, against the Enemies of my Native Countrey. You speak Reason, said the Emperor, and I wish with all my Soul I could advise any manner or way, that you might be able to assist it; but you having told me of your dear Platonick Friend the Duchess of Newcastle and of her good and profitable Counsels, I would desire you to send for her Soul, and conferr with her about this business.

The Empress was very glad of this motion of the Emperor, and immediately sent for the Soul of the said Duchess, which in a minute waited on her Majesty. Then the Empress declared to her the grievance and sadness of her mind, and how much she was troubled and afflicted at the News brought her by the Immaterial Spirits, desiring the Duchess, if possible, to assist her with the best Counsels she could, that she might shew the greatness of her love and affection which she bore to her Native Countrey. Whereupon the Duchess promised her Majesty to do what lay in her power; and since it was a business of great Importance, she desired some time to consider of it; for, said she, Great Affairs require deep Considerations; which the Empress willingly allowed her. And after the Duchess had considered some little time, she desired the Empress to send some of her Syrens or Mear men, to see what passages they could find out of the Blazing-World, into the World she came from; for, said she, if there be a passage for a Ship to come out of that World into this; then certainly there may also a Ship pass thorow the same passage out of this World into that. Hereupon the Mear- or Fish-men were sent out; who being many in number, employ'd all their industry, and did swim several ways; at last having found out the passage, they returned to the Empress, and told her, That as their Blazing World had but one Emperor, one Government, one Religion, and one Language, so there was but one Passage into that World, which was so little, that no Vessel bigger than a Packet-Boat could go thorow; neither was that Passage always open, but sometimes quite frozen up. At which Relation both the Empress and Duchess seemed somewhat troubled, fearing that this would perhaps be an hindrance or obstruction to their Design.

At last the Duchess desired the Empress to send for her Ship-wrights, and all her Architects, which were Giants; who being called, the Duchess told them how some in her own World had been so ingenious, as to contrive Ships that could swim under Water, and asked, Whether they could do the like? The Giants answered, They had never heard of that Invention; nevertheless, they would try what might be done by Art, and spare no labour or industry to find it out. In the mean time, while both the Empress and Duchess were in a serious Counsel, after many debates, the Duchess desired but a few Ships to transport some of the Bird-, Worm- and Bear-men: Alas! said the Empress, What can such sorts of Men do in the other World? especially so few? They will be soon destroyed, for a Musket will destroy numbers of Birds in one shot. The Duchess said, I desire your Majesty will have but a little patience, and relie upon my advice, and you shall not fail to save your own Native Country, and in a manner become a Mistress of all that World you came from. The Empress, who loved the Duchess as her own Soul, did so; the Giants returned soon after, and told her Majesty, that they had found out the Art which the Duchess had mentioned, to make such Ships as could swim under water; which the Empress and Duchess were both very glad at, and when the Ships were made ready, the Duchess told the Empress, that it was requisite that her Majesty should go her self in body, as well as in Soul; but I, said she, can onely wait on your Majesty after a Spiritual manner, that is, with my Soul. Your Soul, said the Empress, shall live with my Soul, in my Body; for I shall onely desire your Counsel and Advice.

Then said the Duchess, Your Majesty must command a great number of your Fish-men to wait on your Ships; for you know that your Ships are not made for Cannons, and therefore are no ways serviceable in War; for though by the help of your Engines, they can drive on, and your Fish-men may by the help of Chains and Ropes, draw them which way they will, to make them go on, or flye back, yet not so as to fight: And though your Ships be of Gold, and cannot be shot thorow, but onely bruised and battered; yet the Enemy will assault and enter them, and take them as Prizes; wherefore your Fish-men must do you Service instead of Cannons. But how, said the Empress, can the Fish-men do me service against an Enemy, without Cannons and all sorts of Arms? That is the reason, answered the Duchess, that I would have numbers of Fish-men, for they shall destroy all your Enemies Ships, before they can come near you. The Empress asked in what manner that could be? Thus, answered the Duchess: Your Majesty must send a number of Worm-men to the Burning-Mountains (for you have good store of them in the Blazing-World) which must get a great quantity of the Fire-stone, whose property, you know, is, that it burns so long as it is wet; and the Ships in the other World being all made of Wood, they may by that means set them all on fire; and if you can but destroy their Ships, and hinder their Navigation, you will be Mistress of all that World, by reason most parts thereof cannot live without Navigation. Besides, said she, the Fire-stone will serve you instead of Light or Torches; for you know, that the World you are going into, is dark at nights (especially if there be no Moon-shine, or if the Moon be overshadowed by Clouds) and not so full of Blazing-Stars as this World is, which make as great a light in the absence of the Sun, as the Sun doth when it is present; for that World hath but little blinking Stars, which make more shadows then light, and are onely able to draw up Vapours from the Earth, but not to rarifie or clarifie them, or to convert them into serene air.

This Advice of the Duchess was very much approved; and joyfully embraced by the Empress, who forthwith sent her Worm-men to get a good quantity of the mentioned Fire-stone. She also commanded numbers of Fish-men to wait on her under Water, and Bird-men to wait on her in the Air; and Bear- and Worm-men to wait on her in Ships, according to the Duchess's advice; and indeed the Bear-men were as serviceable to her, as the North Star; but the Bird-men would often rest themselves upon the

Deck of the Ships; neither would the Empress, being of a sweet and noble Nature, suffer that they should tire or weary themselves by long flights; for though by Land they did often fly out of one Countrey into another, yet they did rest in some Woods, or on some Grounds, especially at night, when it was their sleeping time: And therefore the Empress was forced to take a great many Ships along with her, both for transporting those several sorts of her loyal and serviceable Subjects, and to carry provisions for them: Besides, she was so wearied with the Petitions of several others of her Subjects who desired to wait on her Majesty, that she could not possibly deny them all; for some would rather chuse to be drowned, then not tender their duty to her.

Thus after all things were made fit and ready, the Empress began her Journey; I cannot properly say, she set Sail, by reason in some Part, as in the passage between the two Worlds (which yet was but short) the Ships were drawn under water by the Fish-men with Golden Chains, so that they had no need of Sails there, nor of any other Arts, but onely to keep out water from entering into the Ships, and to give or make so much Air as would serve, for breath or respiration, those Land-Animals that were in the Ships; which the Giants had so Artificially contrived, that they which were therein, found no inconveniency at all: And after they had passed the Icy Sea, the Golden Ships appeared above Water, and so went on until they came near the Kingdom that was the Empress's Native Countrey; where the Bear-men through their Telescopes discovered a great number of Ships which had beset all that Kingdom, well rigg'd and mann'd.

The Empress before she came in sight of the Enemy, sent some of her Fish- and Bird-men to bring her intelligence of their Fleet; and hearing of their number, their station and posture, she gave order that when it was Night, her Bird-men should carry in their beeks some of the mentioned Fire-stones, with the tops thereof wetted; and the Fish-men should carry them likewise, and hold them out of the Water; for they were cut in the form of Torches or Candles, and being many thousands, made a terrible shew; for it appear'd as if all the Air and Sea had been of a Flaming-Fire; and all that were upon the Sea, or near it, did verily believe, the time of Judgment, or the Last Day was come, which made them all fall down, and Pray.

At the break of Day, the Empress commanded those Lights to be put out, and then the Naval Forces of the Enemy perceived nothing but a

Number of Ships without Sails, Guns, Arms, and other Instruments of War; which Ships seemed to swim of themselves, without any help or assistance: which sight put them into a great amaze; neither could they perceive that those Ships were of Gold, by reason the Empress had caused them all to be coloured black, or with a dark colour; so that the natural colour of the Gold could not be perceived through the artificial colour of the paint, no not by the best Telescopes. All which put the Enemies Fleet into such a fright at night, and to such wonder in the morning, or at day-time, that they know not what to judg or make of them; for they know neither what Ships they were, nor what Party they belonged to, insomuch that they had no power to stir.

In the mean while, the Empress knowing the Colours of her own Country, sent a Letter to their General, and the rest of the chief Commanders, to let them know, that she was a great and powerful Princess, and came to assist them against their Enemies: wherefore she desired they should declare themselves, when they would have her help and assistance.

Hereupon a Councel was called, and the business debated; but there were so many cross and different Opinions, that they could not suddenly resolve what answer to send the Empress; at which she grew angry, insomuch that she resolved to return into her Blazing-World, without giving any assistance to her Countrymen: but the Duchess of Newcastle intreated her Majesty to abate her passion; for, said she, Great Councels are most commonly slow, because many men have many several Opinions: besides, every Councellor striving to be the wisest, makes long speeches, and raise many doubts, which cause retardments. If I had long-speeched Councellors, replied the Empress, I would hang them, by reason they give more Words, then Advice. The Duchess answered, That her Majesty should not be angry, but consider the differences of that and her Blazing-World; for, said she, they are not both alike; but there are grosser and duller understandings in this, than in the Blazing-World.

At last a Messenger came out, who returned the Empress thanks for her kind proffer, but desired withal, to know from whence she came, and how, and in what manner her assistance could be serviceable to them? The Empress answered, That she was not bound to tell them whence she came; but as for the manner of her assistance, I will appear, said she, to your Navy in a splendorous Light, surrounded with Fire. The Messenger asked at what time they should expect her coming? I'le be with you, answered the Empress, about one of the Clock at night. With this report the Messenger returned; which made both the poor Councellors and Seamen much afraid; but yet they longed for the time to behold this strange sight.

The appointed hour being come, the Empress appear'd with Garments made of the Star-stone, and was born or supported above the Water, upon the Fish-mens heads and backs, so that she seemed to walk upon the face of the Water, and the Bird- and Fish-men carried the Fire-stone, lighted both in the Air, and above the Waters.

Which sight, when her Country-men perceived at a distance, their hearts began to tremble; but coming something nearer, she left her Torches, and appeared onely in her Garments of Light, like an Angel, or some Deity, and all kneeled down before her, and worshipped her with all submission and reverence: But the Empress would not come nearer than at such a distance where her voice might be generally heard, by reason she would not have that any of her Accoustrements should be perceived, but the splendor thereof; and when she was come so near that her voice could be heard and understood by all, she made this following Speech:

Dear Country-men, for so you are, although you know me not; I being a Native of this Kingdom, and hearing that most part of this World had resolved to make Warr against it, and sought to destroy it, at least to weaken its Naval Force and Power, have made a Voyage out of another World, to lend you my assistance against your Enemies. I come not to make bargains with you, or to regard my own Interest more than your Safety; but I intend to make you the most powerful Nation of this World, and therefore I have chosen rather to quit my own Tranquility, Riches and Pleasure, than suffer you to be ruined and destroyed. All the Return I desire, is but your grateful acknowledgment, and to declare my Power, Love and Loyalty to my Native Country: for, although I am now a Great and Absolute Princess, and Empress of a whole World, yet I acknowledg, that once I was a Subject of this Kingdom, which is but a small part of this World; and therefore I will have you undoubtedly believe, that I shall destroy all your Enemies before this following Night, I mean those which trouble you by Sea; and if you have any by Land, assure your self I shall also give you my assistance against them, and make you triumph over all that seek your Ruine and Destruction.

Upon this Declaration of the Empress, when both the General, and all the Commanders in their several Ships, had return'd their humble and hearty Thanks to Her Majesty for so great a favour to them, she took her leave, and departed to her own Ships. But, good Lord! what several Opinions and Judgments did this produce in the minds of her Countrymen! some said she was an Angel; others, she was a sorceress; some believed her a Goddess; others said the Devil deluded them in the shape of a fine Lady.

The morning after, when the Navies were to fight, the Empress appear'd upon the face of the Waters, dress'd in her Imperial Robes, which were all of Diamonds and Carbuncles; in one hand she held a Buckler, made of one intire Carbuncle; and in the other hand a Spear of one intire Diamond; on her head she had a Cap of Diamonds, and just upon the top of the Crown, was a Starr made of the Starr-stone, mentioned heretofore; and a Half-Moon made of the same Stone, was placed on her forehead; all her other Garments were of several sorts of precious Jewels; and having given her Fish-men directions how to destroy the Enemies of her Native Country, she proceeded to effect her design. The Fish-men were to carry the Fire-stones in cases of Diamonds (for the Diamonds in the Blazing-World, are in splendor so far beyond the Diamonds of this World, as Peble-stones are to the best sort of this Worlds Diamonds) and to uncase or uncover those Fire-stones no sooner but when they were just under the Enemis Ships, or close at their sides, and then to wet them, and set their Ships on fire; which was no sooner done, but all the Enemie's Fleet was of a Flaming fire; and coming to the place where the Powder was, it streight blew them up; so that all the several Navies of the Enemies, were destroyed in a short time: which when her Countrymen did see, they all cried out with one voice, That she was an Angel sent from God to deliver them out of the hands of their Enemies: Neither would she return into the Blazing-World, until she had forced all the rest of the World to submit to that same Nation.

In the mean time, the General of all their Naval Forces, sent to their soveraign to acquaint him with their miraculous Delivery and Conquest, and with the Empress's design of making him the most powerful Monarch of all that World. After a short time, the Empress sent her self, to the soveraign of that Nation to know in what she could be serviceable to him; who returning her many thanks, both for her assistance against his

Enemies, and her kind proffer to do him further service for the good and benefit of his Nations (for he was King over several Kingdoms) sent her word, that although she did partly destroy his Enemies by Sea, yet, they were so powerful, that they did hinder the Trade and Traffick of his Dominions. To which the Empress returned this answer, That she would burn and sink all those Ships that would not pay him Tribute; and forthwith sent to all the Neighbouring Nations, who had any Traffick by Sea, desiring them to pay Tribute to the King and soveraign of that Nation where she was born; But they denied it with great scorn. Whereupon, she immediately commanded her Fish-men, to destroy all strangers Ships that traffick'd on the Seas; which they did according to the Empress's Command; and when the Neighbouring Nations and Kingdoms perceived her power, they were so discomposed in their affairs and designs, that they knew not what to do: At last they sent to the Empress, and desired to treat with her, but could get no other conditions then to submit and pay Tribute to the said King and soveraign of her Native Country, otherwise, she was resolved to ruin all their Trade and Traffick by burning their Ships. Long was this Treaty, but in fine, they could obtain nothing, so that at last they were inforced to submit; by which the King of the mentioned Nations became absolute Master of the Seas, and consequently of that World; by reason, as I mentioned heretofore, the several Nations of that World could not well live without Traffick and Commerce, by Sea, as well as by Land.

But after a short time, those Neighbouring Nations finding themselves so much inslaved, that they were hardly able to peep out of their own Dominions without a chargeable Tribute, they all agreed to join again their Forces against the King and soveraign of the said Dominions; which when the Empress receiv'd notice of, she sent out her Fish-men to destroy, as they had done before, the remainder of all their Naval Power, by which they were soon forced again to submit, except some Nations which could live without Foreign Traffick, and some whose Trade and Traffick was meerly by Land; these would no ways be Tributary to the mentioned King. The Empress sent them word, That in case they did not submit to him, she intended to fire all their Towns and Cities, and reduce them by force, to what they would not yield with a good will. But they rejected and scorned her Majesties Message, which provoked her anger so much, that she resolved to send her Bird- and Worm-men thither, with order to begin first with their smaller Towns, and set them on fire (for she was loath to make more spoil then she was forced to do) and if they remain'd still obstinate in their resolutions, to destroy also their greater Cities. The onely difficulty was, how to convey the Worm-men conveniently to those places; but they desired that her Majesty would but set them upon any part of the Earth of those Nations, and they could travel within the Earth as easily, and as nimbly as men upon the face of the Earth; which the Empress did according to their desire.

But before both the Bird- and Worm-men began their journey, the Empress commanded the Bear-men to view through their Telescopes what Towns and Cities those were that would not submit; and having a full information thereof, she instructed the Bird- and Bear-men what Towns they should begin withal; in the mean while she sent to all the Princes and soveraigns of those Nations, to let them know that she would give them a proof of her Power, and check their Obstinacies by burning some of their smaller Towns; and if they continued still in their Obstinate Resolutions, that she would convert their smaller Loss into a Total Ruin. she also commanded her Bird-men to make their flight at night, lest they be perceived. At last when both the Bird- and Worm-men came to the designed places, the Worm-men laid some Fire-stones under the Foundation of every House, and the Bird-men placed some at the tops of them, so that both by rain, and by some other moisture within the Earth, the stones could not fail of burning. The Bird-men in the mean time having learned some few words of their Language, told them, That the next time it did rain, their Towns would be all on fire; at which they were amaz'd to hear Men speak in the air; but withall they laughed when they heard them say that rain should fire their Towns; knowing that the effect of Water was to quench, not produce Fire.

At last a rain came, and upon a sudden all their Houses appeared of a flaming Fire; and the more Water there was poured on them, the more they did flame and burn; which struck such a Fright and Terror into all the Neighbouring Cities, Nations and Kingdoms, that for fear the like should happen to them, they and all the rest of the parts of that World, granted the Empress's desire, and submitted to the Monarch and sovereign of her Native Countery, the King of Esfi; save one, which having seldom or never any rain, but onely dews, which would soon be spent in a great fire, slighted her Power: The Empress being desirous to make it stoop as well as the rest, knew that every year it was watered by a flowing Tide, which lasted some Weeks; and although their Houses stood high from the ground, yet they were built upon Supporters which were fixt into the ground. Wherefore she commanded both her Bird- and Worm-men to lay some of the Fire-stones at the bottom of those Supporters, and when the Tide came in, all their Houses were of a Fire, which did so rarifie the Water, that the Tide was soon turn'd into a Vapour, and this Vapour again into Air; which caused not onely a destruction of their Houses, but also a general barrenness over all their Countrey that year, and forced them to submit, as well as the rest of the World had done.

Thus the Empress did not onely save her Native Country, but made it the Absolute Monarchy of all that World; and both the effects of her Power and her Beauty, did kindle a great desire in all the greatest Princes to see her; who hearing that she was resolved to return into her own Blazing-World, they all entreated the favour, that they might wait on her Majesty before she went. The Empress sent word, That she should be glad to grant their Requests; but having no other place of Reception for them, she desired that they would be pleased to come into the open Seas with their Ships, and make a Circle of a pretty large compass, and then her own Ships should meet them, and close up the Circle, and she would present her self to the view of all those that came to see her: Which Answer was joyfully received by all the mentioned Princes, who came, some sooner, and some later, each according to the distance of his Countrey, and the length of the voyage. And being all met in the form and manner aforesaid, the Empress appeared upon the face of the Water in her Imperial Robes; in some part of her hair, near her face, she had placed some of the Starr-Stone, which added such a luster and glory to it, that it caused a great admiration in all that were present, who believed her to be some Celestial Creature, or rather an uncreated Goddess, and they all had a desire to worship her; for surely, said they, no mortal creature can have such a splendid and transcendent beauty, nor can any have so great a power as she has, to walk upon the Waters, and to destroy whatever she pleases, not onely whole Nations, but a whole World.

The Empress expressed to her own Countrymen, who were also her Interpreters to the rest of the Princes that were present, That she would give them an Entertainment at the darkest time of Night: Which being come, the Fire-Stones were lighted, which made both Air and Seas appear of a bright shining flame, insomuch that they put all Spectators into an extream fright, who verily believed they should all be destroyed; which the Empress perceiving, caused all the Lights of the Fire-Stones to be put out, and onely shewed her self in her Garments of Light. The Bird-men carried her upon their backs into the Air, and there she appear'd as glorious as the Sun. Then she was set down upon the Seas again, and presently there was heard the most melodious and sweetest Consort of Voices, as ever was heard out of the Seas, which was made by the Fish-men; this Consort was answered by another, made by the Bird-men in the Air, so that it seem'd as if Sea and Air had spoke, and answered each other by way of Singing-Dialogues, or after the manner of those Playes that are acted by singing-Voices.

But when it was upon break of day, the Empress ended her Entertainment, and at full day-light all the Princes perceived that she went into the Ship wherein the Prince and Monarch of her Native Country was, the King of Esfi, with whom she had several Conferences; and having assured Him of the readiness of her Assistance whensoever he required it, telling Him withal, That she wanted no Intelligence, she went forth again upon the Waters, and being in the midst of the Circle made by those Ships that were present, she desired them to draw somewhat nearer, that they might hear her speak; which being done, she declared her self in this following manner:

Great, Heroick, and Famous Monarchs, I come hither to assist the King of Esfi against his Enemies, He being unjustly assaulted by many several Nations, which would fain take away His Hereditary Rights, and Prerogatives of the Narrow Seas; at which Unjustice, Heaven was much displeased, and for the Injuries He received from His Enemies, rewarded Him with an Absolute Power, so that now he is become the Head-Monarch of all this World; which Power, though you may envy, yet you can no wayes hinder Him; for all those that endeavour to resist His Power, shall onely get Loss for their Labour, and no Victory for their Profit. Wherefore my advice to you all is, To pay him Tribute justly and truly, that you may live Peaceably and Happily, and be rewarded with the Blessings of Heaven: which I wish you from my Soul.

After the Empress had thus finished her Speech to the Princes of the several Nations of that World, she desired that in their Ships might fall back; which being done, her own Fleet came into the Circle, without any visible assistance of Sails or Tide; and her self being entred into her own

Ship, the whole Fleet sunk immediately into the bottom of the Seas, and left all the Spectators in a deep amazement; neither would she suffer any of her Ships to come above the Waters, until she arrived into the Blazing-World.

In time of the Voyage, both the Empress's and the Duchess's Soul, were very gay and merry; and sometimes they would converse very seriously with each other. Amongst the rest of their discourses, the Duchess said, she wondred much at one thing, which was, That since her Majesty had found out a passage out of the Blazing-World, into the World she came from, she did not enrich that part of the World where she was born, at least her own Family, though she had enough to enrich the whole World. The Empress's Soul answered, That she loved her Native Countrey, and her own Family, as well as any Creature could do; and that this was the reason why she would not enrich them: for, said she, not only particular Families or Nations, but all the World, their Natures are such, that much Gold, and great store of Riches, makes them mad; insomuch as they endeavour to destroy each other for Gold or Riches sake. The reason thereof is, said the Duchess, that they have too little Gold and Riches, which makes them so eager to have it. No, replied the Empress's Soul, their particular Covetousness, is beyond all the wealth of the richest World, and the more Riches they have, the more Covetous they are; for their Covetousness is Infinite. But, said she, I would there could a Passage be found out of the Blazing-World, into the World whence you came, and I would willingly give you as much Riches as you desir'd. The Duchess's Soul gave her Majesty humble thanks for her great Favour; and told her, that she was not covetous, nor desir'd any more wealth than what her Lord and Husband had before the Civil-Warrs. Neither, said she, should I desire it for my own, but my Lord's Posterities sake. Well, said the Empress, I'le command my Fish-men to use all their Skill and Industry to find out a Passage into that World which your Lord and Husband is in. I do verily believe, answered the Duchess, that there will be no Passage found into that World; but if there were any, I should not Petition your Majesty for Gold and Jewels, but only for the Elixir that grows in the midst of the Golden Sands, for to preserve Life and Health; but without a Passage, it is impossible to carry away any of it: for, whatsoever is Material, cannot travel like Immaterial Beings, such as Souls and Spirits are. Neither do Souls require any such thing that might revive them, or prolong their

Lives, by reason they are unalterable: for, were Souls like Bodies, then my Soul might have had the benefit of that Natural Elixir that grows in your Blazing-World. I wish earnestly, said the Empress, that a Passage might be found, and then both your Lord and your self, should neither want Wealth, nor Long-life: nay, I love you so well, that I would make you as Great and Powerful a Monarchess, as I am of the Blazing-World. The Duchess's Soul humbly thank'd her Majesty, and told her, That she acknowledged and esteemed her Love beyond all things that are in Nature.

After this Discourse, they had many other Conferences, which for brevity's sake I'le forbear to rehearse. At last, after several Questions which the Empress's Soul asked the Duchess, she desired to know the reason why she did take such delight, when she was joyned to her Body, in being singular both in Accoustrements, Behaviour, and Discourse? The Duchess's Soul answered, she confessed that it was extravagant, and beyond what was usual and ordinary: but yet her ambition being such, that she would not be like others in any thing, if it were possible, I endeavour, said she, to be as singular as I can: for, it argues but a mean Nature, to imitate others: and though I do not love to be imitated, if I can possibly avoid it; yet, rather than imitate others, I should chuse to be imitated by others: for my Nature is such, that I had rather appear worse in Singularity, than better in the Mode. If you were not a great Lady, replied the Empress, you would never pass in the World for a wise Lady: for, the World would say, your Singularities are Vanities. The Duchess's Soul answered, she did not at all regard the Censure of this, or any other Age, concerning Vanities: but, said she, neither this present, nor any of the future Ages, can or will truly say, that I am not Vertuous and Chast: for I am confident, all that were, or are acquainted with me, and all the Servants which ever I had, will or can upon their oaths declare my actions no otherwise than Vertuous: and certainly, there's none even of the meanest Degree, which have not their Spies and Witnesses, much more those of the Nobler sort, which seldom or never are without Attendants; so that their Faults (if they have any) will easily be known, and as easily be divulged. Wherefore, happy are those Natures that are Honest, Vertuous, and Noble; not only happy to themselves, but happy to their Families. But, said the Empress, if you glory so much in your Honesty and Vertue, how comes it that you plead for Dishonest and Wicked persons, in your Writings? The Duchess answered, It was only to shew her Wit, not her Nature.

At last the Empress arrived into the Blazing-World, and coming to her Imperial Palace, you may sooner imagine than expect that I should express the joy which the Emperor had at her safe return; for he loved her beyond his Soul; and there was no love lost, for the Empress equal'd his Affection with no less love to him. After the time of rejoicing with each other, the Duchess's Soul begg'd leave to return to her Noble Lord: But the Emperor desired, that before she departed, she would see how he had employed his time in the Empress's absence; for he had built Stables and Riding-Houses, and desired to have Horses of Manage, such as, according to the Empress's Relation, the Duke of Newcastlehad: The Emperor enquired of the Duchess, the Form and Structure of her Lord and Husband's Stables and Riding-House. The Duchess answer'd his Majesty, That they were but plain and ordinary; but, said she, had my Lord Wealth, I am sure he would not spare it, in rendring his Buildings as Noble as could be made. Hereupon the Emperor shewed the Duchess the Stables he had built, which were most stately and magnificent; among the rest, there was one double Stable that held a Hundred Horses on a side, the main Building was of Gold, lined with several sorts of precious Materials; the Roof was Arched with Agats, the sides of the Walls were lined with Cornelian, the Floor was paved with Amber, the Mangers were Mother of Pearl; the Pillars, as also the middle Isle or Walk of the Stables, were of Crystal; the Front and Gate was of Turquois, most neatly cut and carved. The Riding-House was lined with Saphirs, Topases, and the like; the Floor was all of Golden-Sand so finely sifted, that it was extreamly soft, and not in the least hurtful to the Horses feet, and the Door and Frontispiece was of Emeralds curiously carved.

After the view of these Glorious and Magnificent Buildings, which the Duchess's Soul was much delighted withall, she resolved to take her leave; but the Emperor desired her to stay yet some short time more, for they both loved her company so well, that they were unwilling to have her depart so soon: several Conferences and Discourses pass'd between them; amongst the rest, the Emperor desir'd her advice how to set up a Theatre for Plays. The Duchess confessed her Ignorance in this Art, telling his Majesty that she knew nothing of erecting Theatres or Scenes, but what she had by an Immaterial Observation, when she was with the Empress's Soul in the chief City of E. Entring into one of their Theatres, whereof the Empress could give as much account to his Majesty, as her self. But both the Emperor and the Empress told the Duchess, That she could give directions how to make Plays. The Duchess answered, That she had as little skill to form a Play after the Mode, as she had to paint or make a Scene for shew. But you have made Plays, replied the Empress: Yes, answered the Duchess, I intended them for Plays; but the Wits of these present times condemned them as uncapable of being represented or acted, because they were not made up according to the Rules of Art; though I dare say, That the Descriptions are as good as any they have writ. The Emperor asked, Whether the Property of Plays were not to describe the several Humours, Actions and Fortunes of Mankind? 'Tis so, answered the Duchess. Why then, replied the Emperor, the natural Humours, Actions and Fortunes of Mankind, are not done by the Rules of Art: But, said the Duchess, it is the Art and Method of our Wits to despise all Descriptions of Wit, Humour, Actions and Fortunes that are without such Artificial Rules. The Emperor asked, Are those good Plays that are made so Methodically and Artificially? The Duchess answer'd, They were Good according to the Judgment of the Age, or Mode of the Nation, but not according to her Judgment: for truly, said she, in my Opinion, their Plays will prove a Nursery of whining Lovers, and not an Academy or School for Wise, Witty, Noble and well-behaved men. But I, replied the Emperor, desire such a Theatre as may make wise Men; and will have such Descriptions as are Natural, not Artificial. If your Majesty be of that Opinion, said the Duchess's Soul, then my Playes may be acted in your Blazing-World, when they cannot be acted in the Blinking-World of Wit; and the next time I come to visit your Majesty, I shall endeavour to order your Majesty's Theatre, to present such Playes as my Wit is capable to make. Then the Empress told the Duchess, That she loved a foolish Farse added to a wise Play. The Duchess answered, That no World in Nature had fitter Creatures for it than the Blazing-World: for, said she, the Lowse-men, the Bird-men, the Spider- and Fox-men, the Ape-men and Satyrs appear in a Farse extraordinary pleasant.

 Hereupon both the Emperor and Empress intreated the Duchess's Soul to stay so long with them, till she had ordered her Theatre, and made Playes and Farses fit for them; for they onely wanted that sort of Recreation: but the Duchess's Soul begg'd their Majesties to give her leave to go into her Native World; for she long'd to be with her dear Lord and Husband, promising, that after a short time she would return again.

Which being granted, though with much difficulty, she took her leave with all Civility and Respect, and so departed from their Majesties.

After the Duchess's return into her own body, she entertained her Lord (when he was pleased to hear such kind of Discourses) with Foreign Relations; but he was never displeased to hear of the Empress's kind Commendations, and of the Characters she was pleased to give of him to the Emperor. Amongst other Relations, she told him all what had past between the Empress, and the several Monarchs of that World whither she went with the Empress; and how she had subdued them to pay Tribute and Homage to the Monarch of that Nation or Kingdom to which she owed both her Birth and Education. she also related to her Lord what Magnificent Stables and Riding-Houses the Emperor had built, and what fine Horses were in the Blazing-World, of several shapes and sizes, and how exact their shapes were in each sort, and of many various Colours, and fine Marks, as if they had been painted by Art, with such Coats or Skins, that they had a far greater gloss and smoothness than Satin; and were there but a passage out of the Blazing-World into this, said she, you should not onely have some of those Horses, but such Materials as the Emperor has, to build your Stables and Riding-Houses withall; and so much Gold, that I should never repine at your Noble and Generous Gifts. The Duke smilingly answered her, That he was sorry there was no Passage between those two Worlds; but, said he, I have always found an Obstruction to my Good Fortunes.

One time the Duchess chanced to discourse with some of her acquaintance, of the Empress of the Blazing-World, who asked her what Pastimes and Recreations her Majesty did most delight in? The Duchess answered, That she spent most of her time in the study of Natural Causes and Effects, which was her chief delight and pastime; and that she loved to discourse sometimes with the most Learned persons of that World: And to please the Emperor and his Nobles, who were all of the Royal Race, she went often abroad to take the air, but seldom in the day-time, always at night, if it might be called Night; for, said she, the Nights there, are as light as Days, by reason of the numerous Blazing-Stars, which are very splendorous, onely their Light is whiter than the Sun's Light; and as the Sun's Light is hot, so their Light is cool; not so cool as our twinkling Starr-light, nor is their Sun-light so hot as ours, but more rate: And that part of the Blazing-World where the Empress resides, is always clear, and never subject to any Storms, Tempests, Fogs or Mists, but has onely refreshing-Dews that nourish the Earth: The air of it is sweet and temperate, and, as I said before, as much light in the Sun's absence, as in its presence, which makes that time we call Night, more pleasant there than the Day: And sometimes the Empress goes abroad by Water in Barges, sometimes by Land in Chariots, and sometimes on Horse-back; her Royal Chariots are very Glorious, the Body is one intire green Diamond; the four small Pillars that bear up the Top-cover, are four white Diamonds, cut in the form thereof; the top or roof of the Chariot, is one intire blew Diamond, and at the four corners are great springs of Rubies; the Seat is made of Cloth of Gold, stuffed with Ambergreece beaten small: the Chariot is drawn by Twelve Unicorns, whose Trappings are all Chains of Pearl; and as for her Barges, they are onely of Gold. Her Guard of State (for she needs none for security, there being no Rebels or Enemies) consists of Giants, but they seldom wait on their Majesties abroad, because their extraordinary height and bigness does hinder their prospect. Her Entertainment when she is upon the Water, is the Musick of the Fish- and Bird-men; and by Land are Horse and Foot-matches; for the Empress takes much delight in making Race-matches with the Emperor, and the Nobility; some Races are between the Fox- and Ape-men, which sometimes the Satyrs strive to outrun; and some are between the Spider-men and Lice-men. Also there are several Flight-matches, between the several sorts of Bird-men, and the several sorts of Fly-men; and swimming-matches, between the several sorts of Fish-men. The Emperor, Empress, and their Nobles, take also great delight to have Collations; for in the Blazing-World, there are most delicious Fruits of all sorts, and some such as in this World were never seen nor tasted; for there are most tempting sorts of Fruit: After their Collations are ended, they Dance; and if they be upon the Water, they dance upon the Water, there lying so many Fish-men so close and thick together, as they can dance very evenly and easily upon their backs, and need not fear drowning. Their Musick, both Vocal and Instrumental, is according to their several places: Upon the Water, it is of Water-Instruments, as shells filled with Water, and so moved by Art, which is a very sweet and delightful harmony; and those Dances which they dance upon the Water, are, for the most part, such as we in this World call swimming-Dances, where they do not lift up their feet high: In Lawns, or upon Plains, they have Wind-Instruments, but much better than those in our World: And when they dance in the Woods, they have Horn-Instruments, which although they are of a sort of Wind-Instruments, yet they are of another Fashion than the former: In their Houses they have such Instruments as are somewhat like our Viols, Violins, Theorboes, Lutes, Citherins, Gittars, Harpsichords, and the like; but yet so far beyond them, that the difference cannot well be exprest; and as their places of Dancing, and their Musick is different, so is their manner or way of Dancing. In these and the like Recreations, the Emperor, Empress, and the Nobility pass their time.

## The Epilogue to the Reader.

By this Poetical Description, you may perceive, that my ambition is not onely to be Empress, but Authoress of a whole World; and that the Worlds I have made, both the Blazing- and the other Philosophical World, mentioned in the first part of this Description, are framed and composed of the most pure, that is, the Rational parts of Matter, which are the parts of my Mind; which Creation was more easily and suddenly effected, than the Conquests of the two famous Monarchs of the World. Alexander and Cesar. Neither have I made such disturbances, and caused so many dissolutions of particulars, otherwise named deaths, as they did; for I have destroyed but some few men in a little Boat, which dyed through the extremity of cold, and that by the hand of Justice, which was necessitated to punish their crime of stealing away a young and beauteous Lady. And in the formation of those Worlds, I take more delight and glory, then ever Alexander or Cesar did in conquering this terrestrial world; and though I have made my Blazing-World a Peaceable World, allowing it but one Religion, one Language, and one Government; yet could I make another World, as full of Factions, Divisions and Warrs, as this is of Peace and Tranquility; and the Rational figures of my Mind might express as much courage to fight, as Hector and Achilles had; and be as wise as Nestor, as; Eloquent as Ulysses, and be as beautiful as Hellen. But I esteeming Peace before Warr, Wit before Policy, Honesty before Beauty; instead of the figures of Alexander, Cesar, Hector, Achilles, Nestor, Ulysses, Hellen, &c. chose rather the figure of Honest Margaret Newcastle, which now I would not change for all this Terrestrial World; and if any should like the World I have made, and be willing to be my Subjects, they may imagine themselves such, and they are such, I mean in their Minds, Fancies or Imaginations; but if they cannot endure to be Subjects, they may create Worlds of their own, and Govern themselves as they please. But yet let them have a care, not to prove unjust Usurpers, and to rob me of mine: for, concerning the Philosophical-world, I am Empress of it my self; and as for the Blazing-World, it having an Empress already, who rules it with great Wisdom and Conduct, which Empress is my dear Platonick Friend; I shall never prove so unjust, treacherous and unworthy to her, as to disturb her Government, much less to depose her from her Imperial Throne, for the sake of any other, but rather chuse to create another World for another Friend.

FINIS.

CPSIA information can be obtained
at www.ICGtesting.com
Printed in the USA
LVHW100549261022
731591LV00006B/203